T0062997

BOOKS BY ELIZABETH COOKE

Life Savors – A Memoir
Eye of the Beholder
A Shadow Romance
There's a Small Hotel, (Winner Paris Book
Festival 2015 for General Fiction)
Secrets of a Small Hotel
The Hotel Next Door
A Tale of Two Hotels
Rendezvous at a Small Hotel
Intrigue at a Small Hotel, (Winner Grand
Prize Paris Book Festival 2016)
The Hotel Marcel Dining Club – By Invitation Only
How to Game People Without Even Trying – A Daughter's Legacy
Still Life – A Love Story
<u>The Rose Trilogy</u>
Violet Rose – The Encroaching Sea
Starfish – The Arbitrary Ocean
Violet – The Swelling Tide

www.elizabethcookebooks.com

Violet

The Swelling Tide

Elizabeth Cooke

abbott press

This is a work of fiction. All of the characters, names, incidents, organizations, and dialogue in this novel are either the products of the author's imagination or are used fictitiously.

Abbott Press books may be ordered through booksellers or by contacting:

Abbott Press
1663 Liberty Drive
Bloomington, IN 47403
www.abbottpress.com
Phone: 1 (866) 697-5310

ISBN: 978-1-4582-2145-2 (sc)
ISBN: 978-1-4582-2144-5 (hc)
ISBN: 978-1-4582-2143-8 (e)

Library of Congress Control Number: 2017916333

Print information available on the last page.

Abbott Press rev. date: 10/26/2017

PREAMBLE

In book one, entitled **VIOLET ROSE** - The Encroaching Sea - Bud Rose and his beloved, Violet, encounter danger and lust. Bud's illegitimate daughter, Starfish, becomes part of their lives. Malevolent storms beset them, both in tempests of weather and anguish of heart, as the encroaching sea sweeps across their world.

In book two, **STARFISH** – The Arbitrary Ocean - the lives of Bud and Violet Rose and Starfish are filled with drama, as Bud, now a Deputy Sheriff of Suffolk County, pursues a drug cartel plaguing the community. Much of the action takes place in Montauk, a hamlet on the southern fork of Long Island. There is deception and intrigue, identities hidden, and narrow escapes. Throughout, the turbulent ocean mirrors the upheaval and violence the characters encounter.

VIOLET - The Swelling Tide - is the third and final volume in The Rose Trilogy. It continues the story of Bud and Violet Rose with the little girl they call Starfish. Set again on the East End of Long Island in a resort town, the animosity between summer visitor and local resident is vividly depicted, and Deputy Sheriff Bud Rose's continued pursuit of a drug lord turns lethal.

POSTSCRIPT

It is **VIOLET**, the finale of the trilogy that brings the three books to conclusion. **VIOLET** is not the name of a girl or a small velvety flower. It is the most lethal storm to hit Long Island, designated that pretty name by the Federal Weather Service. No shrinking violet is this tempest, as it engulfs the East Coast with devastating consequences to all in its path.

PROLOGUE

There was much on Deputy Sheriff Bud Rose's agenda that November of 1985.

First, he had to find a place to live, since his home on Shore Road in Remsenburg, at the edge of Moriches Bay, had been wiped away in a vicious storm.

Second, he continued the pursuit of the head of a drug cartel that had decimated the youth on Long Island, a Manhattanite named John Grunwald, with a house in Montauk and an apartment in Trump Tower.

Third, he was determined to bring to justice Jillian Burns, his ex-lover and biological mother of Starfish, and her cohort Sasha Annas, Violet's brother. The two had been involved in numerous crimes, the last of which was the actual pushing of drugs.

Then, there were Violet's parents, George Annas and Anastasia! And poor Stella Burns, Jillian's mother, all people who had to deal with the realization that Sasha Annas and Jillian Burns had actually survived the storm, ROSE, and had created ersatz lives and phony identities on the south-easternmost tip of Long Island!

Bud Rose, a rather stoic character, was more than uncomfortable in highly emotionally charged situations. He did not look forward to the scenes to come; and come they would, like torrents of water, that threatened to drown all he knew and loved.

Highest on his list of important *raison d'êtres*, was Starfish - Starfish, and his dear wife, Violet. The two females, one grown, one still an infant in 1985, were the center of his universe, beloved and cherished in a way he could never have expected. The depth of his feelings was a constant astonishment to him, and his sense of protectiveness touched his soul.

For them, he was willing to give his life.

Chapter One

THE HOUSE ON THE HILL

After the loss of their house on Shore Road during the 1985 November storm, Bud and Violet, with baby Starfish, lived in a motel off of Montauk Highway, situated just before the turn into Westhampton Beach proper. It was not ideal, but they shared two rooms for the weeks they spent looking for a property to buy.

Long Island was flat with few hills, but at least a knoll or two. At the western end of Remsenburg, there was one such hillock, at the top of which stood a shingled white house. At one time, it had belonged to P.J. Wodehouse and his wife.

At the rear of the acre on which the house stood, but still on the small hill in the center of the hamlet, was a guesthouse, now separate from the property line. It was particularly appealing to Violet because it was not directly next to a bay. She felt she had been burned by the sea. She knew cement stanchions would not be necessary here to keep the building above water. It was planted safely on grassy ground. It even had a basement.

Through Brandeis Realty, Violet and Bud Rose made a proper, sober offer for what they called The House on the Hill. The Flood Insurance they had for the house on Shore Road was helpful. It made for a quick financial transaction for the purchase.

"Dry land," said Bud. "What a relief…not to have to wrestle with the ocean – with its spilling over Dune Road and right into our living room!"

"Thank goodness," Violet responded. "I remember sitting at the table in the house on Shore Road. It was raining outside and the tide was high. We were eating oysters with a spicy sauce, and suddenly I felt a tingle. My bare feet were wet. The water was several inches across the floor."

"Remember that was before we put four eight-foot stanchions under the house to lift it."

"You're right...but I still can never forget it. It was like an early realization of what the ocean can do. And of course, what it eventually did – take our little house out to sea."

"Well, no more. It's not our worry now," Bud said, resolutely. "Hopefully, those days are gone. We've got our new House on the Hill to keep us dry."

They were able to move in at Christmas time in 1985. Starfish had just turned one year old.

Of course, their new life there was only the beginning of an easier relationship with swelling tides, but by no means the end.

Violet had secured The House on the Hill for a good price. In recent months, her tenure at Brandeis Realty in Westhampton Beach had become much more intense with responsibilities of importance in realty terms. The fact was, Violet Rose was virtually running the office in Westhampton Beach, as Bethany Brandeis was now deeply entrenched in the Montauk branch of her company.

Bethany was also deeply entrenched in one Augustus Brandt, a lawyer for the firm, Montauk resident, and formidable lover.

Violet Rose was thriving as Manager of the Main Street, Westhampton Beach office. Bud Rose was proud of his wife. "You are one impressive lady," he would say to her.

"You just love my commissions," she would respond, laughing.

"No, darling. I love the whole little parcel," and he would take her in his arms and whisper, "every little bit of you." That was enough to end the conversation and take them both to a different place – in the bedroom.

The House on the Hill was filled with music. There was a pine tree set up in the corner of the living room near the fireplace, with a number of bright packages beneath. The boughs had strings of lights festooned, but there were yet to be decorations hanging from the limbs.

Violet was waiting for Bud to come home and help her with that task as she, and baby Starfish, sat on the new red couch before the tree, basking in the sparks that seemed to fly from its lighted, delightful-smelling arms.

Mookie, the dog, was at their feet.

Mookie was a German Shepherd, three years old, that Bud and Violet had adopted from The Bide-A-Wee Home, situated north of Old Montauk Highway. Bide-A-Wee, a no-kill animal shelter and adoption center, with branches in Wantagh and in New York City, was on a one hundred fifty acre piece of land, donated to the animal charity by P.J. Wodehouse in the 1950s.

When Lena James, the young girl handler of Mookie at the shelter had brought the dog out of his cage to meet the family for the first time, Bud Rose fell in love with the animal.

It was reciprocated. The dog ran to the Deputy Sheriff and sat at his feet, adoring eyes fixated on Bud's. That did it. "We have to have him," Bud said.

"You sure?" was Violet's response. "He certainly is big."

"Yeah, but look how gentle. Besides, he is great protection. This kind of dog intimidates – just by the sight of him."

"True," she nodded. "What do you think, Starfish?" The baby gurgled happily.

"It seems appropriate – since we have the Wodehouse guest house as our home, to have a dog that was saved on Wodehouse property," Bud said, and the deal was done. Mookie was now Mookie Rose.

Bud loved the animal, felt him the ultimate police dog, and indeed, he was devoted and loyal to Bud. Bud Rose was Mookie's 'person'.

But he loved his mistress, Violet, as well, and was protective of the child, Starfish. The little one was quite afraid of the big dog. Wanting to play, he would chase after her. Starfish would cry salty tears as he would stand beside her, wagging his tail. Then he would lick her cheek, which only made her cry harder.

(It took a couple of years and a growth-spurt in Starfish before she came to love the dog as much as he loved her.)

Bud finally arrived home. It was near 6:00 PM. "What a day," he announced to his young wife and baby, patting the dog's head as he leapt with joy at seeing his 'person' – "I'm beat."

"Oh, Bud. Come sit here with us," Violet said patting the sofa cushions. "Is it Grunwald again?"

Bud nodded. As Deputy Sheriff of Suffolk County, he, and his department in Riverhead, were determined to apprehend the drug lord John Grunwald. The Deputy Sheriff was also particularly dedicated to catching Jillian Burns and Sasha Annas, pawns in the game of narcotics, yet eager pushers of the illegal product for money, but the apprehension of Grunwald had become Bud's mission.

"The destruction of young lives out here on Long Island …the lethal affects of the 'business' of getting high for a price…the price in dollars… the price in addiction…the price in death…" Bud sat down on the couch and took Starfish in his arms.

"I check John Grunwald's office in Trump Tower on a regular basis," he continued. "I always get the same answer. 'Mr. Grunwald is on business out of the country.' 'When do you expect him back? I always ask.' 'He has not informed us, but surely not for some time,' is the response, every time I call. It's frustrating."

Although Bud Rose was a tired policeman, the sight of his favorite people – and dog – in all the world - raised his spirits. He got up and poured some Merlot from the bar cart in the corner of the room for Violet and himself, sat on the floor next to Mookie who sniffed his glass, and opened the packing boxes, which contained the Christmas ornaments. "Let's decorate!" he announced with a big grin

Laying Starfish on the couch cushions, Violet joined her husband on the floor. They counted out the small treasures in the box from their first Christmas.

Violet was wearing the starfish pin in gold that Bud had given her, his earliest demonstration of love for her. It was at the neck of her cashmere sweater. She unpinned the little brooch, got up, and placed it on the tip of the center branch of the pine tree. "This belongs here," she said proudly, "because Starfish is the center of everything."

"What about me?" Bud said with a grin.

"Oh you. Who are you?" she laughed and ran over and embraced her husband as he sat on the hardwood floor.

Chapter Two

NYC APARTMENT – 114TH STREET

Jillian Burns and Sasha Annas, last seen during the November storm, headed to New York City in an old, green Chevy, had finally landed in an apartment at 114th Street off Broadway on the upper West side of that fabled city.

From their window in the rented space, Jillian could see the Hudson River, down to the left. The building was on a hill that she bitterly resented walking, particularly in the winter wind with the icy blast off the river.

She found it strange that she was still with Sasha. They were tied together by illegal bonds – their own misdeeds and no marriage-license – the latter being all right with her because, in spite of their interdependence, there was little love…even in bed…especially in bed!

In no way did she want to be Sasha's wife. For Jillian, there was still only one man who commanded her every emotion – from passion, sexual obsession, to hate that tore at her heart like acid – the whole spectrum. She realized there was only one key to Bud Rose – the little girl, Rose Bud, Jillian and he had produced out of wedlock and in secret. At that time, her paramour never even knew about the birth.

But Bud Rose certainly knew it now!

'For god's sake! Do they still call her Starfish?' she ruminated. 'She's

Rose Bud! Named for her daddy, Bud Rose. There's got to be a way,' and in her misery, Jillian rolled over and buried herself in her pillow.

She had arrived with Sasha at this place only two days before. They were exhausted and disoriented. After sleeping away the hours, both awoke to the reality of their situation.

"Sasha, who are we now?" Jillian asked, rousing up, tousled, rubbing her eyes. "Scarlet? Alistair? Or good old Jillian and Sasha?"

He was next to her in the bed in the cramped bedroom on 114th Street.

"What's our name? How are we going to get a job? Money?" she continued. "How are we going to live?" The last words were said in a voice of despair. Jillian sank down beside him. "How much cash is there left?"

"Some," he mumbled. Not enough."

"I kept one Jillian Burns credit card –a Visa - Is there any way to use that?"

"Maybe. Let me think about it." Sasha got up and went into the bathroom. On his return, he said, "Jobs are the most important thing – for both of us. I have my old driver's license, as an ID card. Course the Chevy is registered to Alistair Williams."

"Can we still just keep it downstairs parked on the street?"

"Let's hope so. Where else? A garage? Too expensive at the moment." He sat down beside her. "But your credit card. I wonder if the police…"

"You mean Bud Rose, right?"

"Yeah. The ubiquitous Bud Rose!"

"Mom told me he just came into the city to talk to the New York PD about that drug cartel person, but he was not looking for us. Didn't know we were here."

"Yeah but your mother told him you always wanted to go to New York. What's to stop him from nosing around in the city? Bud Rose is pretty tenacious."

"But Mom only said that MAYBE I had come here…to New York City. She certainly left it up in the air."

There was a long pause, each puzzling over their predicament. "You know, that Visa card of mine," Jillian began. "Mom has one with the same number, but in her name. I got a second card for her when I was living and working down in Westhampton, and she was taking care of the baby up in East Moriches. She could take care of Rose Bud's necessities with it, her food and little garments and stuff."

Sasha perked up. "You know, you may have something there. We could call Stella and if anyone questions her about the use of the card – thinking it might be you – she could always say you had left your card with her a long time ago and she used it by mistake."

"But used in New York? She never comes here."

"Maybe Stella could explain she came into the city to see a sick friend." Sasha tossed off this remark with a snicker. "Most important thing is we need to get jobs!"

Jillian had quit using the red dye. She had decided to let her hair grow long and go back to its natural brown. As the days went on and after frequent hair-washings, it began to darken. "I'm Jillian Burns once more," she said proudly, as she inspected herself in the mirror of the medicine cabinet.

And Sasha? His gray streaks began to be overcome by darker roots, but he did not shave off the moustache. He was not quite through with his Alistair persona. Although the hair on his head went through a slowly fading gray-tipped look, quickly enough, its normal dark color returned.

The apartment began to close in on both of them. It was shabby at best, but at least a haven for the moment. Jillian and Sasha began at snap at one another. It was not a happy time.

"It's hard to believe Christmas is only a couple of days off," Jillian complained.

"God, you're always carping."

"And why not? This place stinks."

Sasha had never raised his hand to Jillian, but as he stood over her now, as she sat on an old club chair in the tiny living room, he was ready to do so.

"You are one woman who's really hard to take."

"And I suppose you think you're something special, easy to live with, loveable! Hah. Well, have another think coming. You're rude and mean."

"And you need me, Jillian. You'd be dead if I hadn't pulled you out of that car. I wish I hadn't," he said through clenched teeth. Then whirling around, he grabbed his coat off a chair and headed for the front door.

"Where you going?"

"Out. Anywhere to be away from you," and Sasha slammed the door behind him.

Jillian sat there for a moment, then in the smallest voice, said "Merry Christmas, Mom. Merry Christmas, Rose Bud." She burst into tears. "And god damn you Bud Rose. God damn you Violet Rose. Next year I'll be celebrating a different kind of Christmas. I'll have my daughter with me. Just wait and see. She's mine. She's the only thing I have in my whole life. Rose Bud."

With that, Jillian, hugging herself, gave in to a paroxysm of sobs, her body contorted, twisted, the emotion sweeping over her in waves of tidal strength.

When Sasha returned after midnight, chilled and a little drunk, he found Jillian in fetal position, out cold on the living room rug.

Chapter Three

CHRISTMAS DINNER

Early on that fateful November 1st afternoon, before Violet's confrontation with Jillian over Starfish, as the first windy, rain filled clouds of the storm that moved in, which later claimed the house on Shore Road, Violet had called her father to let him know that his son, her own brother, was alive. Bud's revelation, the night before, of Sasha's survival from the storm, ROSE, had chilled Violet to the bone.

Sasha was her brother, yes. They had always had a conflicted relationship. Was she happy he had lived? Of course, she guessed, or was she just happy he was still alive because she was supposed to be.

"Sasha didn't die, Dad," she said to her father on the phone. She could hear him choke.

"What?" He finally said. "You telling me Sasha's alive?"

"Yes, Dad. Bud discovered him in Montauk – in disguise."

"What do you mean 'in disguise'?"

"New Name. And Jillian Burns was with him. She survived too."

"You're kidding. THAT Jillian Burns? Bud's…"

"That Jillian Burns, Dad. 'Fraid so."

There was silence until, in slow tones he asked, "Sasha didn't drown?"

"No. He managed to get out of the car when it turned over in the surf."

"How come? How was that possible?"

"I don't know," she replied, "but he did, Dad. Sasha's alive."

She heard the phone go dead.

She assumed her father was so moved he could no longer continue. In truth, George Annas had felt one of the stilts supporting his house tip as this latest storm moved in. 'Jeez,' George had thought. 'Is this the one that takes me down?' And he had run to the door and down the swaying steps to see the damage to the structure below, Sasha for the moment forgotten.

⋆⇒◈⇐⋆

That was then. This was now, Christmas day, 1985 with a turkey in the oven in The House on the Hill. The aroma of stuffing with sage and giblets filled the house as an excited one-year-old girl pulled at colored tissue wrapped packages, a family gathered, and a dog barked with delight.

It was not a large group gathered there under the tree, with Bloody Marys all around. George and Anastasia Annas, Violet's parents, and of course Bud and Violet. All four were in festive mood. Joe and Alice Rose, the Deputy Sheriff's parents had moved to New Haven, Alice's hometown, to be with her ailing mother. Bud had called them earlier to wish them Happy Holidays.

Bud had also called Stella Burns to wish her the same. She was grandmother to Starfish, and he felt obligated to do so. In the course of their conversation, he asked Stella if she had heard anything from Jillian. The answer was she had not, although Bud was dubious with this response. He never trusted Stella. After all, she was Jillian's mother. Her loyalties were in question.

George Annas was regaling the little audience with tales of the stilt house.

"You know, that storm, the first of November, well, it almost took the house. Fortunately, two of the stilts held. The other two hit the sand. God, the place was tilted crazy."

"How'd you live there?" Violet wanted to know.

"You know your father, Violet. He immediately went out and got four metal stanchions," Anastasia interjected.

"Not stanchions, Ana, poles. Four metal poles."

11

"Okay. Poles," she said with a smile.

"I propped up the house and you know? It's good as new." George Annas lifted his glass. "To stilts! Whether wooden or metal."

"Metal's best," said his wife demurely.

George turned his attention to the child at his feet. "And you, my little Starfish. I want you to come over and swim to your heart's content – any time – any day."

"She sure loves the water," Violet said.

"I noticed, and as her Grandpa, I'll be there to guard her good and watch her take to the waves."

Violet rose to her feet, went to the kitchen, returning quickly with the announcement, "Turkey time." For all, it was a swift exit to the dining room.

They were hungry.

Chapter Four

A MONTAUK HIDEAWAY

There were different kinds of Christmases, just as there were different kinds of real estate for Bud and Violet Rose, Jillian Burns and Sasha Annas, and even for Bethany Brandeis and Gus Brandt.

The latter two had grown seriously involved, particularly on Bethany's side. She was determined to keep her eager lover as long as possible, even into a marital state, although that was the least essential motive for her purchase of a very special property.

She wanted a place of their own, for making love. How Gus pleased her! Gus made her ecstatic over and over again. This feeling Bethany Brandeis never wanted to be without, so she went ahead, unbeknownst to Gus, and bought the perfect *venue*.

It was a small, saltbox, shingled house right out of the 18th century or a Hopper painting. Sitting on a hill, opposite the beach and limpid ocean, it took a staircase to wind up the hill, to a path to the entrance. Through bayberry bushes, and Montauk daisies, one came to a portico covered in vines. Beneath it was the front door, painted the color of the sea.

There was a living room, not large, but with a window overlooking the water below, where Bethany put sofas covered in white linen. She had hand painted doors with floral motifs installed. Gracing the walls were early American primitive paintings. There was a quantity of seashells, coral, turtle shells as accents about the room, and there was a fireplace on an angle in the corner, the mantle made of gray stones. The tiny kitchen next door had an old-fashioned black-iron stove.

Somehow, it reminded one of an elegant ship, with its pine paneling. Up a small set of stairs was the only bedroom. The brass bed was set in a bay window. It seemed to hover over the ocean below, truly a bed for dreams.

Bethany Brandeis had bought the place, rationalizing it was an excellent investment, so private, so unusual in this world of mansions, and so unique and charming. But really, she had to admit to herself, she had purchased this property she dubbed The Cove as a trysting place for her and Gus Brandt.

Bethany was in love big time! The Cove was her Christmas present to Gus and herself. She planned a major 'unveiling' for him on New Year's Eve when they could drink the year 1986 in, with champagne and caviar. In the brass bed in the bay window upstairs, they could drink of each other – all night long - welcoming the New Year in a state of ecstasy.

"Happy New Year, darling," were the first words Bethany heard as 1985 turned into1986, uttered by Gus in the brass bed, a true 'bed for dreams'. She turned to him and everything started all over again, just as she had hoped.

Bethany, although distracted beyond reason with her love affair, was still a realtor at heart. Her business in Montauk was hugely successful. She had had to hire two extra agents because of the large traffic. The cold winter days might be slower, but the minute the month of March came around with the promise of summer, the clients would be breaking down her doors at the office on The Circle.

She was thankful for Violet Rose. There, too, in Westhampton Beach, the business of selling and renting real estate was increasing. Bethany was in contact with Violet daily – by phone – but realized, that as the owner of the company, she would have to spend more time in the older office in the near future because of the extra traffic.

Gus would understand. Or would he?

When she broached the subject to him, that she planned to spend more time out of Montauk, west of the hamlet, he at first seemed annoyed. "Then why'd you buy this house?"

"It has nothing to do with that, Gus. It's just that the Westhampton Beach office is a little short-handed and with spring approaching, I will have to hire new people to cover the clients and that means training them…"

"You'll be staying over at night, I presume?"

"Yes," she said. "I still have the old house on Mill Road. It's not much, but it's close to the Westhampton Beach office."

He was grumpy. She could tell by the turn of his mouth.

On the following Monday, the beginning of January in the new year, as Bethany was loading her car to head back to Westhampton Beach, Gus helping her in the driveway, he looked down toward the water below, so clean and fresh. "Wow. It's beautiful here. And what a super clear day… the air…very bracing."

"I wish I could stay to enjoy it," she said, coming toward him.

"Yeah, well you'll be back…"

"Soon, darling." She reached up to kiss him. She caught his cheek with her lips. "Are you driving back to your office now?"

He shook his head. "No. I don't think so. Think I'll stay here for a while. In fact, I think I'll stay here at night regularly. Too pretty to miss – and you know my stuffy old apartment. This is much better…grander."

Bethany could only nod in agreement. As she got in the front seat of her car, she had a disconcerting feeling that she was leaving an unresolved situation. She did not know what it meant, but Gus apparently was moving into The Cove with or without her.

As she drove west, she brushed the feeling aside, but it did not go away. It haunted her. The Cove was for the twosome. The Cove was for them.

"It's a love nest," she said out loud. "He'll be there alone. He'd BETTER be there alone." She shook her head to dispel the thought. "Don't let jealousy rouse its ugly head," she continued talking to herself, "but that was one lousy kiss goodbye!" And she put her foot to the pedal and sped up Montauk Highway toward Westhampton Beach and her old home.

Chapter Five

COOP

For Jillian and Sasha, it had been a bleak Christmas. The day went by with little notice. The two did treat themselves to a dinner at a small bar named Gallagher's on Broadway near 102nd Street. There, they had drinks (several) and a dinner of roast chicken. That was it. No presents. No decorations. (No money!)

The tab was paid with Jillian's Visa card.

Jobs were uppermost in both their minds. Jillian considered her options. Any real position would require her SSN, perhaps a *resumé*, references, even a tax return. She managed to write out a reference from The Suffolk County Air Base Storage Facility, where she had worked in Westhampton Beach three years earlier. Sasha took it to a Kinkos, nearby on Broadway, to have it typed out and Xeroxes made.

He also wrote his own reference from King Kullen where he had worked for some years as Assistant Manager. He had copies made of this too.

Armed with her reference documents, Jillian found a job as receptionist/ticket taker at a movie theater near 110th Street. In her little glass cage at the entrance, she doled out tickets for a price and was meticulous in counting the money and turning it in. Jillian began to feel safe for the first time in months, her small, enclosed cubicle giving a false sense of security.

Sasha's job hunt took a bit longer, but in two weeks he managed to find a job at Gristedes, an outlet of the grocery chain on Broadway and

98th Street. He was not a bag boy, nor a grocery clerk. He was Assistant at the meat counter where special orders were placed and complaints of customers were handled. The pay wasn't great, but at least, it was regular money coming in. Besides, he thought, with an inner smile of satisfaction, 'nobody's gonna look for me here among the roast beef and pork chops!'

It was tedious, boring work, but a necessity – the money.

Sasha grew friendly with a younger man named Cooper Allison, called Coop. He was ambitious – as was Sasha – always talking of extra jobs – extra cash. Sasha listened.

Coop came to Sasha one day and whispered, "Hey, I've got a deal that might interest you."

Thinking 'drugs', Sasha responded, "I don't think so."

"Hey, hear me out."

They were standing in the actual butchery behind the glass. It smelled of raw meat.

"I got a night job. The pay is intense!" Coop laughed. "I mean really major."

"Yeah?" Sasha said, skeptical.

"It's at Trump Tower. You know, the monster building across town on Fifth Avenue?"

"Sure, I know it."

"Well, I am now the proud employee of room service for the restaurant there, called The Grill. We bring food up to the different apartments when one of the mucky-mucks orders up dinner. Big tips. I mean intense tips!"

Sasha was suddenly all ears. "Yeah?"

"They're looking to hire, Sasha. You'd be ideal. You got that classy moustache and you're always so neat – like a British guy."

That did it. Sasha thought 'I've still got the look,' and the following night, Sasha joined Coop on his way to work at The Grill to apply for a similar job.

He got it.

Chapter Six

BACK IN TOWN

As the cold months passed, Bud Rose, Deputy Sheriff, was frustrated in his efforts on the drug front. He still checked regularly with Trump Tower about the whereabouts of John Grunwald, to no avail. Eldridge had been deposed and was in custody. Joe Grady of Joe's Warm-up Bar was on probation, although still able to operate his bar.

However, the big honcho of the cartel was apparently somewhere still on the continent of Europe.

Although there was much other work for Bud Rose to do, the usual smaller crimes of lust and vengeance, still, the drug scourge, which had turned so deadly, was a mission about which he was passionate.

By springtime, 1986, there was a break. John Grunwald was fed up with Europe. He had been gone from the States for almost six months, since the beginning of November, 1985 It had been a licentious, luxurious, sensual time for him, first at The Crillon in Paris, then at The Palace in St. Moritz, and finally at The Grand Hotel at Cap Ferat.

It was April when he journeyed to the Riviera and The Grand Hotel. The weather was a perfect 78 degrees in the daytime, the mid-40s at night. He was accompanied by 'a sweet, sexy thing with big breasts,' as he was inclined to say. But frankly, the young woman was not very bright and John Grunwald – except for bedtime – was excruciatingly bored.

He missed New York City and the familiarity of his lavish apartment, plus associates and friends who colored his days in that city. 'Ah for a sirloin steak at The 21 Club', he would sigh. 'All this fancy food! Too much, already,' and he dreamt of going home.

So he went. He flew out of Nice, back to the United States, First Class, of course. It was an uneventful journey, but as the hours on the plane passed, he began to realize he might be returning to the very set of problems he had sought to escape. They would not have gone away…the problems with the drug trade.

Finally ensconced in his Trump Tower digs, amidst the gold lacquer and antique mirrors, John Grunwald wrote out a list. There were only four names – three associates in the New York City narcotics trade, and the final one, his Captain Willis. Grunwald needed a source on Long Island. "The city – that's no problem, but I have a lot of customers on the East End," he said out loud, "and I got to have a new supply."

He called all three on the phone, one by one. Each of his colleagues was reticent, but equally, all three had the same reference for an ample source of smack out on Long Island. It was a simple barbershop called The Clipper, located close to the Islip/MacArthur Airport…where the planes come in! "Not boats, this time, John," one of his associates said, "but planes!"

Grunwald got on the telephone again. First, he called Melinda, his sister in Mystic, Connecticut to let her know he was back in New York. Then, he phoned the Captain of his yacht, *The Otellia*. Captain Richard Willis welcomed his boss home.

After amenities, Grunwald asked, "Anything I should know, Richard?"

"Well, things are a bit dicey right now."

"What do you mean?"

"I've been hearing that heroin has gotten so strong, it's lethal."

"We all know it's not all peaches and cream in the trade, Richard. That's nothing new.".

"No. It is new. A friend of mine's father scored a bag and the stuff was so potent, it killed the man."

John Grunwald grunted.

"And that's not all," Richard Willis went on. "A young man in my neighborhood –down at the marina– right across the pier from me, collapsed on the dock and died. I had watched the boy grow up – nice kid…" Richard Willis couldn't continue.

John Grunwald paused. He grew cautious, wary, not an unusual stance for such a man. "What are you trying to say here, Richard?"

"Well, sir, I have always been happy to do the trade…with you, for you…"

"You've certainly been happy with the extra cash!" Grunwald interrupted, his voice harsh.

"Yes. Yes, I have. But now…I've been thinking…"

"Well, stop thinking!" Grunwald almost shouted.

There was silence on the other end. Finally, Captain Richard Willis said quietly, "I can't do it anymore."

"You can't what?"

"You know. Meet the boats with *The Otellia*…off Montauk…make the trade of dollars for packets of White Sugar." He paused. "I just can't do it."

"What are you so scared of? Are you such a weak-kneed coward?"

"No, Mr. Grunwald, but I don't want to get caught and go to jail." There was silence. Then, Richard Willis continued, "Besides – the smack is so strong now – it kills people."

"Boy, you're some lily-livered big disappointment," Grunwald blasted over the phone. "Look, I wooed you away from my friend's yacht to Captain for me – losing that friend in the process. And you've made a lot of money." Then, with a lowered, threatening voice, Grunwald said, "Willis, you owe me!"

There was no answer. "Well?" Grunwald questioned, his voice rising.

"Sorry, Mr. Grunwald, I quit," and the phone went dead.

John Grunwald looked at the empty receiver. He picked up a rare Chinese urn that was on the end of the table and hurled it across the room. It hit a mirror, which crashed to the floor, glass shards spreading out amidst the broken pottery.

The man sat there furious. 'I have a yacht, *The Otellia*,' he thought. 'A yacht without a captain, a yacht without a crew, a crew that knew the drug trade and the waters off the coast of Montauk, where *The Otellia* dominated. Christ. Now what am I gonna do?'

The only other Long Island outpost for narcotics exchange that John Grunwald knew of was out of the small barbershop in Islip, near the Islip/MacArthur airport. It was quite a comedown for the King of Drugs, which he felt himself to be, but it still would keep him in business and might be extremely lucrative. That's all that mattered to him.

"Near the airport," he muttered to himself. "Who needs boats to bring in the stuff when many an airplane is available!" He rose to his feet and started pacing, excited. "Yeah! Old Montauk – where the boats come in. Islip - where planes arrive every hour, every day, from everywhere in the world!" He clapped his hands.

With that, distractedly, John Grunwald picked up the phone and called Housekeeping. "Hey, somebody made a mess up here. One of the maids must have broken a very expensive Ming vase and somehow a mirror. Get someone up here pronto to clean it up."

He sat back in his desk chair, took out a cigarette, lighted it, and picked up a pen. Upon a yellow pad before him, he listed the same three people in the narcotics business that had mentioned the barbershop in Islip. They could give him a name, a connection, the dealer. Then, he made his phone calls. He got what he wanted.

"The Clipper, that's the shop. The dealer, his name is Hal!" John Grunwald sighed with satisfaction. He patted his stomach.

"Okay, Islip, here I come. May the skies stay clear and the planes land safely. John Grunwald will be waiting – with open arms." He leaned back, puffed away on his cigarette, and smiled. "I'm famished," he said out loud, and picked up the phone and called The Grill.

Chapter Seven

SEDUCTION

As Alistair/Sasha brought the steak and baked potato with sour cream/ bacon topping to John Grunwald's apartment from The Grill downstairs in Trump Tower, he had no idea he would come away seduced into a new direction.

"Seen you somewhere," were the first words Grunwald said, as Alistair/Sasha placed the generous tray on the table where the great man was sitting.

"Don't know where that might have been," Alistair/Sasha said with a smile. "*Bon Appetit!*"

"No, no...you...I know I've seen you...maybe out on the Island?"

"Well, I was *Maitre d'* at The Montauk Yacht Club for a couple of summers."

"Yes! That could have been it. I ate there a lot...had a suite at Gurney's Inn before I bought the house on Culloden Point Yes. Definitely. It's... Alistair, isn't it? Am I right?"

"Why, yes. You remember. Thanks."

Grunwald was sawing away at the large steak on the plate before him. "You were a great asset there. What happened? How in hell did you end up here in room service?"

"I hit some bad times," Alistair/Sasha said, shifting his feet, fussing with the salt and pepper on the tray. "Wife...you know...a cheater."

"That's why I never married," Grunwald said with a kind of glee.

"Anyway, I left Long Island – to get a fresh start. My roots are still there."

"I thought you were English," Grunwald said, loudly chewing his steak.

"Well, that's kind of my persona." He blushed. "It helped at The Montauk Yacht Club."

John Grunwald let out a great laugh. "That's rich! You're so right. What snobs. Pretty smart of you, Alistair." He set down his fork. "Now tell me your real name, and where you're really from."

The two men were eye to eye.

"Westhampton Beach. And the name is Sasha Annas. My Dad has a stilt house on Dune Road where I grew up. I worked at King Kullen in Eastport – became Assistant Manager. That's the truth, Mr. Grunwald."

"Westhampton Beach, eh?" Grunwald said chewing away. "You know that part of the Island?"

"Oh, sure. Been there my whole life…as far down as Montauk." Sasha did not go into the car theft business or the White Sugar nonsense. Not now. Not when the intimacy surrounding this moment promised what? A future?

"And up toward Islip? You know that area too?"

""Yeah. Some. My Dad has a car dealership in Westhampton – but he supplies rental cars at the Islip/MacArthur airport."

"As far as Islip, eh? So, you know the Island well, Sasha?"

"Well, at least Suffolk County. I know it as well as anyone, I guess."

John Grunwald rocked back in his chair. "You know, Alistair…I mean Sasha. I just may have a job for you!" With that, he attacked the luscious baked potato adding extra sour cream to the mix and found it absolutely delicious.

Alistair/Sasha was soon to be back in a business that paid off in unexpected ways.

As Sasha left the apartment, he told John Grunwald to just ring down, and he would come back to retrieve the tray.

"Don't worry, Sasha. I know the drill. I'll put the tray out on the floor in front of the door to the hall, okay?"

"Okay, sir."

"We'll speak soon, right?"

"Yes sir." Sasha was elated as he went out into the hall.

As Grunwald sat there at table, he lighted another cigarette. He remembered what he had been told by Eldridge, over at Gurney's Inn. 'The *Maitre d'* at The Montauk Yacht Club – name of Alistair – you can score through him.'

"Yeah," Grunwald said out loud, puffing away. "Alistair – really Sasha. He's my man. He's corruptible!"

Chapter Eight

TOO GOOD TO BE TRUE

"A sea star." Bud was looking at the sand at his feet. He and Violet were sitting together near the ocean's edge at her father's stilt house on Dune Road. It was an early evening in June, 1986. The little girl, Starfish, was on his lap. "Do you see it there, Violet?"

She turned her head. "Sea star?"

"Yes," Bud said. "The starfish – there in the sand. They are sometimes called sea stars. When they sense thunderstorms approaching, they grab hold of many small stones with their five little legs, looking to hold themselves down in the roiling waves as if with anchors."

"Oh, yes. There it is – all golden there," Violet said with a smile. "Like our Starfish - a Sea Star."

Even when very small, when Starfish saw a big wave coming, she would clutch the small rocks that were strewn along the shore and ride out the rush of water. Later, bigger and stronger, she let the muscular ocean waves suck her out, but not too far. It was not a little frightening, but the pulse of the sea and the scent of the briny air thrilled the child.

For Violet, the water was healing. It was freeing, and even though now she lived on high ground since the loss of the Shore Road house to malevolent waves, even though she felt terror at the power of the ocean, she was still part of its primal force.

Sometimes, during an evening swim at her father's house on Dune Road, Starfish by her side, there were shooting stars above the waves, lighting up the sky for a few lingering seconds, then disappearing. Violet would feel an almost religious benediction on both mother and child.

She was a devoted mother. She was also devoted to her real estate business, at which she was becoming quite known for her acumen and honesty in a game that could be murky. Violet's life was full, with a home that she prized, a husband she adored, and a baby girl that was the light of her life.

And a wonderful large and happy dog named Mookie.

It was almost too good to be true.

Bethany Brandeis was impressed with Violet, by her dedication to the business, by the competence and charm with which she ran the Brandeis Realty Office in Westhampton Beach. "You're making us lots of money, sweetheart," Bethany would coo to Violet in there regular phone calls. She genuinely liked the younger woman and her handsome policeman husband, Bud.

It had been infrequent that Bethany actually appeared at the Main Street, Westhampton Beach office. She was anchored in Montauk at the new Brandeis Realty Office on The Circle there. She was delighted, too, with The Cove, her house on the water outside of town, where she and Gus Brandt enjoyed each other to a delirious extent – at least as far as Bethany was concerned. Oh my, she was in love, and the first one to admit it. With the beginning of spring, however, Bethany had come more often to the office over which Violet now presided.

"More customers, you know, need more agents," she exclaimed, and hired a couple of recent graduates from the Riverhead Realty School.

To Violet, Bethany would speak in the most ecstatic tones of her lover. "He takes care of me in I can't tell you the countless ways. I've never had such a lover. He makes me sing…"and on and on, to the point of embarrassment.

"I hope it stays so wonderful," Violet would interject. "I hope he feels the same – that he sings too," she could not help but add.

"Oh, he does. He does. I know he's over the moon," and the conversation would end on this happy note, Violet thankful that it did.

"Too good to be true," Violet would mumble.

At Brandeis Realty, where these conversations took place, Violet was glad to have the privacy of her inner office. Bethany's blandishments about the lawyer, Gus Brandt, were often graphic in describing their sex-play.

"She's besotted," Violet told her husband.

"At least she's getting some work done, apparently. The figures she's pulling in – the commissions – they're sizeable," Bud exclaimed.

"She sure loves that house…the one on the water. She calls it The Cove."

"Maybe we'll get to see it one day."

"It would be fun to pay her a visit. Maybe we can…with Starfish. The Cove is right on the ocean. Our little girl would love it." Violet was getting excited. "She might even find a sea star. I'll ask Bethany if we can come visit next time we speak."

"What about that guy she's with?"

"Oh, I'm sure he's not there all the time."

How wrong a supposition! Grus Brandt moved into The Cove. His clothes were there. His car was parked in the driveway at the back of the house every night. His bottle of scotch was at the ready on the bar, and most of all, Bethany was there as often as she could be, waiting, flushed and eager, any doubts suppressed, never wondering if it all was just too good to be true.

Not for a minute.

Chapter Nine

LENA

Lena, the young blond girl in her late teens, a helper at minimum wage at Bide-A-Wee, who had taken care of Mookie, was particularly appealing to Bud and Violet Rose. Lena's obvious love of the dog touched them.

Violet decided to use Lena as baby-sitter, on occasion, when she was holding an Open House. The girl could surely use the extra money. Anastasia, Violet's mother was able to care for Starfish sometimes but not always. So, as spring turned to summer, Lena became part of the family dynamic.

She had a boy friend. He also worked up at Bide-a-Wee. They were a couple. Neither was particularly outgoing. They found each other in their own quiet way. They were sweet young people, and Violet liked them both, especially Lena. Her young man, sandy haired and a bit clumsy, Violet only knew as Gil. He would drive Lena over to the house and pick her up there when babysitting duties were done.

Did he ever join Lena in those duties in the house? Violet thought it probable, but it did not bother her because Starfish was happy and seemed to be fond of both.

One evening at the beginning of July, returning home late from a dinner with a potential client at Trumpets on the Bay, a fine restaurant in Eastport– Bud had a meeting at his office in Riverhead –Violet found Lena asleep downstairs on the couch in the living room.

When she roused her, she had to shake her hard. Lena was disheveled, the cushions making lines in her cheeks, her hair mussed and hanging with tangles. Lena's eyes were red and she seemed disoriented, groggy, and not making much sense.

Had she been drinking? That was Violet's first thought. As Lena rubbed her eyes, Violet went over and checked the small bar set-up in the corner of the living room. It was untouched and the measurement in the three bottles looked to be where they should be.

"Are you okay?" Violet asked, as she returned to the end of the couch. Lena was sitting there, bleary and unsteady.

"Why sure. Sure I'm okay. Why wouldn't I be?"

"You seem a little out of it."

"Just sleepy, I guess." Lena got up. Violet went to her purse and pulled out some bills. "Thanks, Lena," she said handing the money to the girl. "No problems with Starfish?" this said with a smile.

"There never are," Lena said and headed for the door, jacket in hand. "See you soon. Call me anytime." Violet noticed the girl seemed unsteady.

"Is Gil out there waiting for you?"

Lena just nodded and closed the front door behind her.

Violet went upstairs to the little girl's bedroom. She gazed at the sleeping child with such love suffusing her heart. She stroked her head with its soft, wispy hair, leaned down, kissed her cheek, and went into the adjoining bathroom to turn off the light that Lena had inadvertently left on.

"What the…?" Violet whispered. The place was a mess. There were used tissues on the floor. The wastebasket was turned over, spilling out the contents. The floor next to the tub was wet. On the sink was a half full bottle of Eros, a men's cologne.

Bud never used cologne.

Was Gil here with Lena tonight?

It had occurred to Violet before that Gil might possibly join Lena in her babysitting duties once in a while, but tonight? The two always seemed so quiet, so polite, unassuming. To leave this bathroom in such disarray was out of character.

Violet sank down beside the toilet. She was distressed beyond reason because somehow, she had let someone take care of Starfish who was deceptive and apparently impaired.

'God', Violet thought, 'When I think of it, I noticed last Sunday, after I came back from the Open House on Dune Road, that Lena hadn't closed the freezer door on the refrigerator and a lot of food had melted and had to be thrown out. She must have had a soda and needed ice and just forgot to close it tight.'

Violet got up and stood still, but her thoughts kept moving. 'And two weeks ago, when I had to go to a closing – mid-day – when I came back, Lena was sleeping on my bed – fully dressed - certainly near the baby in her crib – but her mouth was open and – well – it just was so… unprofessional. She seemed so out-of-it.'

As Violet looked about the bathroom, among the spilled contents of the wastebasket, she saw what appeared to be a small plastic bag.

"No!" Violet was horrified. "Could she?" She picked up the slippery item out of the trash on the floor. She had trusted her heart – Starfish – to what? A junky? "This is for Bud," Violet said out loud. "Oh, my God. Is she hooked?"

⊷⧓⊶

When Bud got home near midnight, he found his wife on the living room couch. She was upset, disturbed.

She told him about Lena's discomposure, her vacant stare. "I couldn't believe how weird she was acting. And I remembered other times recently, where she has been so strange."

Then, she turned to her husband who was beside her on the couch. "I think she's using, Bud." She handed him the plastic bag.

He took it, smelled it. "I think you're right."

"I found it in the bathroom – which was a mess – with tissues all over the floor. I had thought at first she'd had drinks, but there was no smell of liquor on her and the bar looked untouched."

Bud was on his feet, plastic bag in hand. "I'll surely get this analyzed," and he put it in a separate paper bag he took from his brief case. "God. Is Starfish all right," he asked.

"Yes, she's fine, thank goodness." Violet paused. "You know what else I found in the john?"

30

Bud shook his head.

"A bottle of men's cologne – with the sexy name of 'Eros'!"

"What? Was her boyfriend here?"

"I don't know, but could be. Why else the cologne? Certainly Lena doesn't use it - or smell of it."

"I never liked the idea of the pair of them, alone here in our house – together – with Starfish."

"Oh, Bud. I feel like such a bad mother…to have let this happen."

"Stop that, Violet. It's not your fault. We knew Lena from Bide-A-Wee. She was a nice young girl, and good with the baby…how could anyone know that she would get sucked in like so many other kids…"

"I'm so sorry for her."

"Well, one thing's a positive. I may be able to get her to tell me where she got the stuff. And more important, from whom?"

Bud Rose, Deputy Sheriff, felt he had a lead to go with and go to. "I'll be up to see Lena at Bide-A-Wee, as soon as I can," he said firmly. "In the meantime, let's find another babysitter." And he kissed his wife.

It took Bud a couple of days before he was able to go to Bide-A-Wee, only to find that Lena had been fired.

'I'm late again,' Bud thought to himself, 'Just like Jillian at Joe's Warm-Up Bar in Montauk. Damn it! What kind of a policeman am I?' Mentally, the Deputy Sheriff was kicking himself.

The girl at the desk in the front room at Bide-A-Wee was busy with papers. There was a small rescue dog – a little mutt – running about in back of her desk at her feet.

"I'm really sorry," the girl said off-handedly, "but Lena began coming in late, and frankly, she just wasn't 'with it' when she was here – sleepy – unfocused. We just couldn't keep her."

"How long has she been gone?"

"Couple of weeks," was the response.

Bud was dismayed. "And Gil? How about him?"

"Oh he's gone too. When she left, he quit."

"Do you have an address?" Bud asked.

"No, just the old one for Lena. I know they went off together, but I don't know where."

Bud was angry in not finding Lena at Bide-A-Wee – that she had been fired – and two weeks earlier. He perked up when Violet gave her husband Lena's home phone number.

"I used it to contact her for babysitting. Don't know if it'll do any good. She may not be there anymore," Violet said as she handed Bud the number on a piece of paper.

She was right. When Bud dialed it, he found the phone no longer in service. "She must have cancelled it because she realized the law would be after her and her addiction," he said, dispirited. "Another dead end!"

He determined to track her down in any case. "She can't have gone too far – and with Gil. Both are from here. A lot of people know them," he said aloud. The Deputy Sheriff, though discouraged, remained undaunted. 'I'll find them', he told himself.

Eventually he did and it wasn't pretty.

Chapter Ten

THE COVE

On one sunny morning, in late July, Bethany found a lady's thong in the brass bed as she was making it. She had thrown back the mussed coverlet and top sheet, and there, at the bottom of the bed was the wisp of black silk.

Bethany did not own a thong.

Her mouth dropped. She and Gus had passed a night of splendid lovemaking and the damn thing was there through it all, right at their feet, during the amorous tussle, the shrieks of delight, the sounds and movement of healthy, unadulterated passion.

She felt sick. With a Bic pen she found on the side table, Bethany hooked the thong and held it at arm's length, as if it were alive. The front panel was of see-through lace, the back only a silken string. She studied this symbol of betrayal for a long moment, as first, tears blurred her vision, then a cold anger started in the pit of her stomach and she blurted out "That bastard!"

She did not want to touch the thong. It was beyond filthy to her. However, she knew she had to retain it somehow as evidence with which to confront one Augustus Brandt, lawyer and lover, now adulterer. Not that they were married. Still her commitment to him had been total. Obviously, his to her was not.

Bethany sank down on the rumpled under-sheet holding the object hanging on the Bic pen as far away as her arm could stretch. For minutes, she could not move. Finally, telling herself to calm down – which was hard – she rose and went to the closet where both she and Gus kept clothes – his on the left, hers on the right. There was an empty shoebox on the floor. Bethany managed to lift the top off and drop the offending underwear into it and replace the top. She kicked the box into a corner on her side of the closet beneath her hanging clothes. "Later," she said grimly, looking at the box. "Later, Gus. You're in for it!" and she slammed the closet door.

Gus had gone to work earlier, after a delicious breakfast of French toast with melted butter and Vermont maple syrup. Over coffee, they had been grinning at each other like two apes, Bethany thought now. And when he left the house for his car on the rear driveway, he had kissed her hard, put his hand under her nightshirt. Then, with a final slap on her bottom, the man went merrily on his way.

"That bastard!" she blurted out loud again as she returned to the disheveled bed and sat upon it. She had to make a plan. This discovery had turned her world upside down. She felt the fool, and for Bethany Brandeis, this was a new feeling, one never felt before, that of self-disgust.

'How stupid have I been! What a silly woman I've become…all over the sexual excitement that man arouses.' She rose to her feet and started pacing. 'I knew it, God damn it, Bethany,' she said to herself. 'I knew it when he told me he was going to live here – move in – because it was so grand, he said. Yeah. Right! He used the place to screw any bimbo he liked when I was out of Montauk.'

"Well," she said decisively to the empty bedroom, "we're going to have an unusual dinner tonight – everything he craves. I'll get lobster and champagne – and he loves *crème brulée*. Oh yes, Gus, it'll be a night to remember!"

With that, Bethany quickly made the bed, finished dressing, gathered her purse and went out to the Lexus at the back of the house. In Montauk proper, she finished her purchases and returned to The Cove. She did not bother to go into her office on The Circle. She did not care about business. Not today. Her focus was on the evening ahead.

Chapter Eleven

ANOTHER CASUALTY

That very July morning when Bethany discovered the thong, Bud Rose had driven into New York City to meet with Flannigan, the head detective with whom the Deputy Sheriff of Suffolk County was collaborating.

Flannigan knew that John Grunwald had returned from Europe and was at his apartment in Trump Tower. He also knew that the alleged drug lord had hired a high-priced lawyer 'just in case', according to an anonymous associate of the magnate.

Flannigan had this day brought Richard Willis, the former Captain of Grunwald's yacht, into the precinct for questioning. He knew the man had left *The Otellia* of his own volition, but the detective wanted to know exactly why – and also what had gone on before he left Grunwald's service.

For this specific moment of truth, Flannigan wanted Bud Rose's participation. Bud had been so close to the Montauk operation that he might be useful.

The Deputy Sheriff was ushered into a small room, the kind with a one-way window. Flannigan and Captain Willis were already seated at a table. With only a bow to Flannigan, Bud took the extra chair.

"It's docked at Mystic Marina, right?" Flannigan's tone was muted.

"I guess so," replied the Captain. The man looked pale, but composed. He sat erect in his plain, dark suit, no Captain's dress. "I quit *The Otellia* a couple of months ago, but my guess is it's still there."

"By the way, this is Deputy Sheriff Bud Rose," the detective said.

"He's out in Suffolk County and as you must know, his jurisdiction goes down as far as Montauk."

"Yes, sir. I know." The Captain gave Bud a tentative smile.

"While you were working for Mr. Grunwald, when you were sailing the yacht off the southern tip of Long Island…?"

"Grunwald had a suite at Gurney's Inn. Then, later, a house on Culloden Point," Willis interrupted.

"And you?"

"I had a small apartment at the marina."

"Except when you sailed, of course," Flannigan said.

"Of course."

"How often did you go out," Bud interjected.

"Depended. Sometimes there was quite a party – maybe six or seven people. We'd go down around the Point to see The Lighthouse. The Inn would supply a grand lunch – with lobster rolls…."

"I've had them," Bud couldn't help but say. "So good."

"There were always lots of drinks."

"And drugs?" Flannigan asked directly.

"No sir. Never. Mr. Grunwald – well he was a drinker – but never touched drugs…not that I know of," Willis quickly added.

"So you were there just to sail a party boat?'

"You could say so."

"Captain Willis, I have to be honest with you. We have a person in custody that has emails and ledgers showing that *The Otellia* was busy on many a night, going out to sea with only you and three crewmembers aboard. No lobster rolls. No liquor. The boat would return to the long pier at the end of Gurney beach after a few hours. It would then unload cardboard boxes and deliver them to the person in question in the garage area of The Inn." Flannigan paused.

During this bit of conversation, Willis had begun to slump in his chair. His head was down. His shoulders sagged.

"Have you anything you want to say?" Flannigan asked, his voice noncommittal. "Now is the time."

Captain Willis cleared his throat. "The person you speak of has to be Martin Eldridge, the Manager of the Inn. He did all the arrangements."

"I can't hear you," Bud said.

"I said it has to be Martin Eldridge."

"And who were these arrangements for? Certainly Mr. Eldridge wasn't selling the contents of those boxes himself, now was he?" Bud continued.

"No. Of course not."

"Then who?"

"Can I get a glass of water?"

"Later," Flannigan said. "Just name the name, Willis. You will only make things easier on yourself."

There was a long pause. "It was my boss. The owner of the yacht, John Grunwald."

"How did it work? You know…the mechanics of the operation," Flannigan asked.

"Eldridge would get an email with instructions. They were curt… just 'pick-up – 8.00 PM tomorrow night off Culloden Point – so many degrees. Or, near The Lighthouse. You know. Location. Direction."

"And who would you meet?"

"Mostly Cubans – little Spanish speaking guys. They had the stuff already in packets – put together back on some Cuban farm, but it was not always Cubans. Sometimes there was a boat from as far north as Canada."

"Kind of an expensive way to operate," was Bud's comment.

"For sure," Willis agreed. "More expensive for the pusher but easier and quicker to distribute – and no middleman."

"So the instructions came from Grunwald?"

Captain Willis nodded.

Flannigan and Bud Rose looked at each other with the same expression that said 'we got him!' Flannigan rose and opened the door. He yelled to someone, "Can we get a glass of water here?" then shut it.

No one spoke for several minutes until the door opened again, and a city cop passed a paper cup full of water to Flannigan who extended it to Captain Willis.

"Thanks. I needed this." He drank. "What happens to me?"

"I would advise getting a lawyer Captain Willis," Flannigan stated.

"You've been most helpful here, so that will be in your favor, but I have to say, you are in deep."

The man was obviously shaken.

"How did you get pulled in?" Bud couldn't help but ask.

"At first I said absolutely not…but then he offered money…I still said no, until the amount he…you know the Godfather phrase… 'he made me an offer I couldn't refuse…'" With that, Captain Willis put his head down on the table.

For the first time, Bud Rose felt sorry for him. He was basically a decent sort. He had fallen victim to a man who wasn't, a bribing son-of-a-bitch who knew how to use and abuse the human weakness in others.

"John Grunwald!" Bud went over and touched the Captain's shoulder. 'Richard Willis, poor sucker. He's just another kind of wreckage in this world of drugs,' Bud thought as he patted the man's shoulder once more.

Chapter Twelve

A PRESENT FOR GUS

That July evening of the same day, Bethany awaited Augustus Brandt. In a silky red caftan, she sat on one of the white sofas in the living room of The Cove. There were candles lighted, a champagne bucket filled with ice and a bottle of the best *Moët Chandon*.

In the refrigerator in the kitchen sat rosy chunks of lobster, greens for a salad in a zip-lock and a Caesar dressing prepared. Two *crème bruleés* in ramekins rested on the sideboard, ready to go under the broiler at the propitious moment to brown the sugary top.

Bethany strolled to the window overlooking the ocean below. The sound of the surf could barely be heard under the voice of the Tony Bennett CD, as he sang "Stranger in Paradise". The tender music brought tears to her eyes, but only for a second, as she whispered, "That bastard."

Gus burst through the front door and into the room behind her. "Hey, hey, baby. What's the occasion?" His voice was ebullient, pleased: the scented candles, the sound of music, the diaphanous red caftan. He could see her figure outlined through it. "Come here, gorgeous."

Bethany turned to him with her best smile. Gus embraced her, but she would not let him kiss her. She couldn't, and quickly whisked away to the champagne bottle. "How about opening this beauty?" And she placed the icy bottle in his outstretched hand.

"Wow. That's cold," he exclaimed.

"Well, shouldn't it be?"

Gus was pouring the sparkling wine into two glasses, as she said, "How was your day?" and lounged back on the sofa.

"The usual." He gave her a glass and sat down beside her, sipping his own. 'Now, tell me. What's the occasion?"

"What do you mean?"

"Well, the candles. The music."

"And lobster in butter sauce for dinner."

"Really? My favorite." He paused. "Is there a reason for all this?"

"Well, yes there is," Bethany said coyly. "In fact, I have a present for you."

"A present?"

"Yes. It's something I know you wanted."

"Well, where is my present, darling?" he asked with a big grin.

"Later. After we eat… and that means I best get to the kitchen." Bethany rose and disappeared into the next room.

Gus took off his jacket, undid his tie and removed it. He was relaxed, comfortable and yes, even excited. 'A present', he thought. 'Now what can she have gotten for me?'

They sat before the fireplace, unlit, at the small dining table with a bowl of roses between them. The lobster was superb (Bethany was one good cook!) and the dessert to his liking.

"This is delicious," he exclaimed. "So creamy."

"Oh, Gus," Bethany asked as he was scooping up the last of the custard. "Do you have the house key on you?"

"Sure. Why? You need it?"

"I do. We came here together yesterday…"

"In separate cars."

"Yes, but I didn't realize I left my key to this house back in Westhampton – stupid mistake."

"We used mine to get in."

"Yes. That's right. The thing is, I'll need your key tomorrow. I'll be in and out of here a lot – have some showings and I hate to leave our lovely love nest unlocked." Bethany was giving him her most seductive eye.

"It's right here," he said, reaching into his trouser pocket and handing his key ring over to Bethany.

"I'll just take it off of this. Your office and car keys are on it too," she said as she carefully removed the bronze-colored key to The Cove. She handed him back the key ring.

"God, Bethany. That was some dinner. Now, it's my present time, don't you think?" Gus was eager, curious. "Has it something to do with this dinner? Is it a trip to Paris for the two of us?"

Bethany laughed. "Why would you think that?"

"Well, the champagne…the *crème brulée*…both pretty French, no?"

"I suppose so. But no, your present is not a trip to Paris. In fact, I'll just go get it." She rose, placing Gus's key to The Cove in her caftan pocket. Actually, her own key to the house was safely housed in her purse in the bedroom.

Bethany went to the far side of the room, and on a small table, behind a club chair, she retrieved the shoebox wrapped in colorful tissue paper. Slowly, she brought it over to him while he still sat at the dining table with its leftover dishes.

Pushing aside the *crème brulée* ramekins, Gus ripped off the paper and opened the shoebox. He was grinning as he did so. He did not realize at first what the bit of black cloth at the bottom of the box was. There was no paper around it. The black thong was there alone.

As he pulled it out of its place of hiding, his jaw dropped. He said nothing but beads of sweat appeared on his brow.

Bethany was standing. She was quiet. Finally, she said to him in her lowest, most mellow tones. "Goodbye, Gus. Leave now. I'll have someone drop your clothes at your office tomorrow."

She turned on her heel and went over to the front door, opening it. It was a beautiful late summer evening. Tony Bennett was still singing, this time "Because of You", which, to Bethany, seemed somehow appropriate.

Gus was still in the chair at the dining table. His face was red. Gradually, he rose, shoving the shoebox and black thong on the table beside the dirty dishes. He went to the sofa and got his jacket, which he slung across his back, holding it with one finger.

As he neared Bethany who held open the front door, he stood and eyed her up and down. "It was a good run, sweetheart, wasn't it?"

As he passed her on his way out, "Hey, you'll still want me as your lawyer…you know business," he said in a tentative voice.

"You've got to be kidding!" Bethany yelled. "Get out!" and she slammed the door behind Gus Brandt, nearly hitting him in the rear end. She waited a moment, crossed the room and blew out the candles one by one, then, as Tony Bennett started in on "The Shadow of your Smile", she fell onto the sofa and burst into tears.

The Cove was hers alone, hers to keep, hers –but oh so empty.

Chapter Thirteen

FAIR IS FAIR

The Clipper was a small barbershop in a strip mall in Ronkonkoma, Town of Islip. It lay on a side street off of Veterans Memorial Highway. From the large front window, you could see, in the distance, the Islip/MacArthur Airport, a busy enough place, taking much of the extra traffic from LaGuardia and JFK.

The Clipper was noisy but very popular. The level of din was high because planes on their descent paths flew low over the barber at work and his customers. The reason the men came there was for Hal, because he was not only an excellent clipper, but he had a humorous, outgoing personality that everyone enjoyed. He was funny, and besides, he had a second, very lucrative business that many appreciated and bought into.

It was to The Clipper that Sasha now made his way in the green Chevy, on his mission for John Grunwald. He easily found the place, parked and entered the small building with its sign engraved on the large front glass window.

"Hi," he said to the man behind a chair trimming the edges of a middle aged, almost bald fellow's hair, what there was of it. "Are you Hal?"

The clipper nodded. "Yeah. I'm Hal."

"Could you do me?"

"Sure. After I'm through here."

It was a late afternoon on a hot day in July, but the barbershop was air-conditioned. It had only three chairs to work. There were a couple of sinks, a door to a back office, and also a rear door to the outside and the back of the mall. From a side window, Sasha could see a stretch of grass and what looked to be a gravel driveway. He could also glimpse a slice of The Islip/MacArthur Airport in the distance – perhaps only four or five miles away.

Sasha sat in one of the chairs that ringed the sidewall. He picked up a magazine, Sports Illustrated, and pretended to read it, but his ears were primed and his senses acute to the atmosphere and to Hal himself. Unfortunately, the sound of a low flying plane drowned out any conversation between Hal and his customer, much to Sasha's dismay, but soon enough, the hair cut was done, paid for, and the man gone. Sasha would have his moment.

"You ready for me?" he inquired.

"Yep, come on over and take yourself a seat." Hal slapped his cutting chair. "I'll only be a moment," and he went into the back room, closed the door. Soon enough he reappeared.

"You're lucky. This is the quietest time of day."

"Really?" Sasha replied. "Why's that?"

"Most of my business comes in after 5:00 r 6:00 – you know, after work."

"Gets crowded, does it?"

"You can say that again," Hal said proudly. He was a man in his late fifties, graying, with a lined face. "How much you want off?"

"Just a trim."

Hal proceeded to move his scissors, lifting small clumps of hair, snipping away happily. He was quite deft in his movements. "What are you doing out here? Going off on a plane? I haven't seen you before."

"No. I'm new to the area. Heard about you," and Sasha turned his head to look directly in Hal's eyes.

"What'd you hear?"

"First, that you were an excellent clipper," Sasha said with a grin.

Hal paused, scissors in air. "And?"

"That maybe you had a second line of business."

Hal said nothing. He got back to clipping. "Who are you, fella? You a cop?"

Sasha burst out laughing. "Good God, no! A cop. *Au contraire!*"

"What's that mean?"

"It means 'on the contrary' in French. No way I'm a cop."

For a moment the two were silent. The only sound was snip, snip, snip. Then, Sasha ventured, "They say, that because you're so close to where the planes come in, you might have access to a contraband of sorts."

Hal did not respond. Then, "you want a hot towel?"

"A hot towel?"

"Yeah, for the face. I'm done with the hair."

"Okay. Why not?"

Hal went to a basin, next to which was a small steamer. He took from it a clean, damp towel and placed it over Sasha's face, covering his eyes. It felt warm and delicious there in the dark. Sasha heard another low flying plane. "The planes come in all day long?"

"Night too," said Hal.

"Make quite a racket," Sasha said.

"That they do. That they do."

Sasha removed the towel. "What I said about contraband...any truth to it?"

"Who wants to know?"

"I do."

"Who are you?"

"Just a guy eager for a source."

"How eager"

"Big bucks eager."

At this crucial moment, two men burst through the front door. They were laughing. "Hey Hal," they called out.

"Here come a couple of regulars," Hal said to Sasha. "I'll be back to you in a sec," and he went forward to meet the pair with a slap on the back of each – a Jimmy and a Steve –and a suggestion, "Just take a chair and I'll be over in a minute.

He returned to Sasha. "Come back with me," and Hal led him into the back room. "Your bill is $15 for the cut and an extra $3 for the towel."

"How much for a packet of contraband?" Sasha said this so directly, Hal blanched.

"Who said I had it?"

"Never mind."

"It's not cheap."

"I'm sure. If it's good stuff, it's expensive. I have a buyer in New York City who would like a reliable supplier – like yourself – on a regular basis. He's wealthy. You could be too, if he's satisfied with the sample."

"You on the up and up?"

"Absolutely."

"Give me your name and how to get a hold of you."

"Sure," said Sasha and handed him a business card that had his name, phone, and title: 'Investment Broker'. He had had the cards made at Kinkos.

"Here's a card for The Clipper," Hal said, handing his to Sasha. "Now, you go outside – I mean all the way to the street and I'll bring you something and we can make the exchange off premises, got it?" Hal was all business.

"Got it," Sasha said and did as he was told. The two met next to the green Chevy.

Finally, Sasha had a packet in his hand and Hal, several hundred dollars in his, a fair exchange.

After all, fair is fair.

Chapter Fourteen

MOTEL 666

In a seedy motel, off Veterans Memorial Highway, Gil and Lena had found haven. It was cheap, and although they did not have much money between them, in the past, they had been able to stash away a sufficient amount to go to Motel 666, and from there, to The Clipper and buy a packet or two.

For the last several weeks, they had been holed up in a rented room at Gil's cousin Jake's. It was a tiny house in Eastport. Lena and Gil were hiding out, because they both realized, their mutual addiction had been made obvious.

At first, when Lena was fired from Bide-A-Wee, Gil was furious with her. "How could you be so stupid?" he yelled at her. "To let it show? To be so bleary?"

Lena, normally quiet, yelled back, "You're just as much in this as I am, Gil."

For the weeks they stayed at Jake's, not going out except to get take-out – Chinese, Pizza, burgers – the two mild young people turned cranky and nasty to each other.

"I'm going stir crazy," Gil would moan. "This place stinks of old food."

Lena was shaky and often in tears. "There's nothing to ease the pain," she would sob.

"You mean, no smack."

"What else?" and she would turn away from him on the bed. Her drug withdrawal was far worse than Gil's.

Finally, by the very end of August, unable to stand the situation any longer, they decided to drive up to Islip, get the usual room at Motel 666 and visit The Clipper.

"Look. It's worth it," Gil said. "I think if enough time goes by, everybody will forget about old Lena and Gil," and the two kissed, packed their meager belongings, said farewell to Jake – with the remark – "who knows? We may be back!"

With that, they were off in Gil's old Buick. It had belonged to his father, who had died three years earlier. It was an old-fashioned car but it still ran and that was all that mattered, and most important, it got them to Motel 666 first – and then The Clipper.

"Christ, I need something," Lena would whimper during the drive.

"Hang in there," Gil would say. "It won't be long."

Soon enough, Gil had set Lena up in the shabby motel room. She lay on the bed, sweating, almost delirious. "Get me some strong stuff," she whispered. "Real strong."

"Will do," Gil replied. "I'm off."

There was no problem with Hal. Gil had been to The Clipper on several occasions. On this visit, he managed to afford three packets – "strong?" – "the strongest" was the answer, and now broke, but satisfied, Gil high-tailed it back the motel stash in hand.

"We'll party tonight," he said with glee to the music on the radio. "How we'll party!"

They did! It was a party to end all parties!

They did not just share a packet. They got just high enough to wish for a second, and after that, well, there was nothing else to do but hit the third and get screaming high.

The finale was Lena, naked on the bed, going limp. Gil, naked, next to her, looked over to her with swimming eyes, "passed out, eh honey?" at which he too went limp and in seconds was snoring away.

It was hours before Gil's eyelids blinked. A dim light was seeping through the venetian blinds at the one small window. His mouth was dry, sour. His head hurt and he was cold, naked there, with the air-conditioner blaring away under the window. Gil tried to pull up a blanket from the end of the bed, but Lena's body lay across the bedclothes.

"Hey. Hey. Lena," Gil said. He touched her arm. "Talk about cold! Hey, move it, will you? I'm freezing."

There was no response.

Gil sat up. He went over and put on his tee shirt, went into the bathroom, and with a towel about his shoulders returned to Lena's side of the bed. He stood there, looking down at the small naked girl, her blond hair strewn about the pillow like strips of butter that seemed to shine in the light from the open bathroom door.

"Hey Lena." Gil prodded her arm again. "I'm cold but you're like ice!" Suddenly he let out a strangled cry. "Lena. Wake up. For Christ's sake, wake up." He was shaking her.

Tears pouring down his face, Gil stepped back in horror. There was only one thing for him to do. He got into his jeans, picked up the small bag he had packed for himself, grabbed his razor and toothbrush from the bathroom, and carrying his shoes, went as quickly as he could to the Buick parked in front of the motel room.

Dawn was just breaking as Gil drove east, back to Jake's. Where else?

Gil could hardly see, as the sun came up. Tears were still flooding his eyes. His heart beat so hard in his chest he felt it would burst. He drove slowly with no wish other than to survive. And Lena? Gone! Over! Done!

Gil was sick inside. He could not bear to picture the dead blond girl on the bed at Motel 666. He pulled over to the side of the road and put his head in his hands, which were wet with tears and sobbed like a baby, shoulders shuddering, a young distraught man disgusted with his own cowardice.

Chapter 15

IN ALL DIRECTIONS

That summer of 1986, Sasha moved out of the apartment on 114th Street. He left to share a place with Coop and split the rent in a brownstone off 96th Street. Coop, the friend he had made at Gristedes, the friend who had enhanced his earning capacity by hooking him up at the Trump Tower Grill, was an easier live-in than Jillian. That woman had begun to drive him nuts.

Sasha not only room-serviced the various duplexes and triplexes at that luxurious Tower on Fifth Avenue, but his hard work and superior attitude had earned him the position of assistant to the Manager of Room Service. Oh, he still delivered, but usually to the highest priced living quarters of the more spectacular inmates of the building.

The tips were great, or 'intense' as Coop would say. Sasha was also performing special duties for John Grunwald on a weekly basis where the money was 'double intense.'

And Jillian? Alone on 114th Street? She was not particularly unhappy Sasha was gone. Any loving feeling between the two was long over, replaced with animosity and a form of disgust, but she WAS lonely. Her job at the theater was pretty boring, although she too had advanced in her duties.

She now worked in the office upstairs. Her pay was higher, and the work on the books more challenging, but she was quite isolated. She missed the bit of banter she had with customers when she was downstairs, doling out tickets from her glass cage.

The Manager of the theater, an Italian guy named Salvatore, only came into the upstairs office a couple of times a day. He usually hung out in the first floor Reception Room.

Jillian did not miss her erstwhile companion, Sasha… not at all. She found it strange, in a way. They had been together for well over a year. They had been through the life-threatening storm ROSE together, changed identities together, pursued jobs under fake personae together, even pushed drugs separately and as a pair.

It was some history, she thought. Still, she did not wonder about Sasha much. Her old obsession with Bud Rose and the baby Rose Bud (Starfish) consumed her as intensely as ever it had. In fact, her loneliness only exacerbated it.

Jillian was in contact with her mother in East Moriches – by phone. There were frequent calls. She would always ask if Stella had received any news of Bud Rose.

"No. We don't socialize," Stella would exclaim.

"I mean, any questions about me?"

"When he calls, he always asks if I've heard from you."

"And?"

"I always say no."

"Thanks, Mom. Let's keep it that way."

Jillian heard her mother heave a sigh of displeasure.

"Well, you don't have to sound so disapproving, Mom," she said angrily.

"I didn't say anything. And you don't need to be so testy, Jill."

There was a long silence.

"Has Bud brought the baby up to see you?"

"Yes, he has. In fact, she was here last week." Stella's voice had lightened. "What a precious little thing. She's got some words now and toddles around. Big smile. Some baby teeth. Bud says she loves to swim."

"She swims?"

"Not really, but she adores the water, sitting on the beach with the waves coming over her tummy."

"Isn't that dangerous?"

"No. No. She goes as often as possible to 'swim' at her Grandpa's house on Dune Road. She loves the feel of the water rising and falling like breath. She floats there among the wind-whipped whitecaps."

"That's crazy!" Jillian was alarmed.

"Bud said Starfish thinks she can see the world as if she was a fish."

"Crazier and crazier," Jillian shouted into the phone.

"No, no. Bud says she's a real little starfish. That's why they call her that."

"She's Rose Bud!" Jillian said, furious. "What a stupid name for a child. Starfish! It's disgusting."

"I think it's kind of cute," said her mother.

That had been the end of their last conversation.

Chapter Sixteen

POOR LITTLE LENA

It was August 31st, when Deputy Sheriff Bud Rose was called to Motel 666, after a maid discovered Lena's body. As leading detective in the drug investigation going on in Suffolk County, Long Island, Bud was the obvious person to handle an OD up near Islip.

The minute he saw the face of the dead girl, after lifting the sheet that covered her body, he recoiled. Babysitter for Starfish. Mookie's handler at Bide-A-Wee. He knew already that it was Lena James. Her wallet with identification and a few dollar bills, plus other possessions, had been left in the room.

To view her pallid face upon the pillow, blond hair spread out in a fan, brought tears to his eyes. 'So young', he thought, 'so very young and such a nice girl'.

In the bathroom, Bud found a bottle of Eros, the men's cologne. Gil had been with her. Gil had left her this way. It was such a cold, unhappy ending, that Bud felt physically sick.

He arranged to have Lena's body taken to the morgue in Riverhead. He would have to find her family, and of course, being the responsible kind, he alone would have to inform her parents personally, a difficult mission to say the least.

Gil! Bud did not have his last name, although the owner of Motel 666 did. Harrison. Gil Harrison. The owner also had further information relevant to the drug investigation. For Bud, it was a bonanza!

"The two have been here several times," the owner told the Deputy Sheriff.

"Really? How often?

"Oh, I'd say, at least once a month over the last year or so."

"Why do you think they came to your place, to Motel 666?"

"Don't know." Bud saw the owner, an overweight fellow in his sixties, start tapping a pencil on the counter in the reception area. He was behind it and appeared suddenly nervous.

"No, honestly," Bud persisted. "Why would they come HERE? To this particular motel?"

"It's cheap."

"Did they go out…to see what? Did they order take-out food?"

"Yeah, they did."

"Come on. Once a month? Did they drive off anywhere?"

"Maybe they were just here – you know – to get away alone – and you know – screw…?"

"Yes. Possibly. But I happen to think there was maybe another reason. The girl OD'd. She OD'd in your motel."

"I know. I know." The man looked anguished. "It's horrible."

"Do you have any idea where and how they got the drugs?" Bud took out his notebook and pen.

"Look. I don't want to get anyone in trouble."

"Seems like you might be in a bit of trouble yourself."

"I don't have anything to do with drugs." The owner's fat cheeks had turned bright red.

"Perhaps not you – but maybe you know of someone who does." Bud paused. "You better tell me. You'll only be helping yourself."

The owner sat down with an 'oof' on the chair behind the counter. It sagged under his weight.

"All I know is that…well, there's this barbershop up in Ronkonkoma – near the airport. I think the guy that runs the place…well, I think he might supply stuff to some of his customers. At least, I've heard tell…" His voice drifted off.

"The name of this place?"

"The Clipper."

"You think that maybe, possibly, Gil Harrison and Lena James, might have gone up there to make a buy?"

The owner just nodded his head.

"And they would come back here to…party?"

He nodded again.

Bud waited a minute. "Do any of your other clients come to Motel 666 for the same reason – because it's close to The Clipper?"

"I guess…maybe."

"That's not an answer."

"Yes!" The owner spat out the single syllable.

"What more do you know about The Clipper, and I'm telling you, sir, that you'd best be honest with the law."

The owner looked subdued. Then, in a low voice, he said "I do know the head guy there is called Hal…that the area is known to have a busy street trade – being so close to the airport."

"What do you mean by 'street trade'?"

"You know…local apartments, even street corners. Many of the dealers are addicted…but not Hal – or so I've heard."

"You seem to have heard quite a lot," Bud said sardonically.

"Yeah." The owner looked quite pleased with this remark.

"And?" Bud continued.

"I don't know much more…except that it's not all a piece of cake. There's a lot of violence – particularly gangs – with guns."

"I don't doubt it," said Bud, closing his notebook. "The Clipper seems to be in the center of quite a hot pocket."

The owner laughed. "Hot pocket! You can say that again."

Chapter Seventeen

SASHA'S NEW GIG

Sasha had been doing regular runs to The Clipper all through August for John Grunwald. At least once a week, he took the green Chevy down to the Ronkonkoma strip mall. Hal, the barbershop/supplier had his business ready and waiting to be transferred in two plain paper bags with a Publix logo emblazoned on each. Sasha would take the bags, in which nearly one thousand small packets of smack were packed - 500 packets in each paper bag - to the trunk of his car.

From there, he would drive very carefully on The Long Island Expressway to the East End and make two deliveries: first, to the owner of an Italian restaurant in the town of Southampton, and the second bag was destined for a fishery plant in Montauk, whose manager enjoyed the fruits of pushing white sugar.

A large amount of cash – always cash – no checks – no letters of intent – strictly cash – was exchanged for the contents of each bag. The dollar bills were placed in those same Publix paper bags, which Sasha took to the trunk of his car. Soon enough, he was back on the highway, headed to Trump tower in New York City with the gelt.

For each mission, Sasha Annas was paid handsomely.

It couldn't last forever.

When Bud had learned of the connection to The Clipper that Gil Harrison and Lena James had formed, in terms of obtaining drugs, he had ordered a stakeout with an Islip policeman at that locale.

Bud had no idea that Sasha Annas was in any way involved, much less that he was a minion of the drug lord, John Grunwald, at least not yet.

These facts would soon enough come to light. The Islip policeman, in an unidentified vehicle, had been on duty for three weeks. He had remarked on a green Chevy that arrived early – near 7:00 AM - when the area was still dead - every Monday morning. The driver would get out of the car, enter the building, and soon return with the owner of The Clipper, the man named Hal. They would each carry a paper bag from Publix, the grocery chain.

Hal would hand the second bag to the driver (actually Sasha) who would open the trunk of his car and place the bags within, then shut it with a clunk. He would then approach Hal, hand him an envelope, get into his car and drive off, toward the Expressway. The whole encounter would take less than five minutes.

The Islip cop called Bud Rose in Riverhead, after three weeks with the same routine, and reported these encounters to the Deputy Sheriff.

"Now were getting somewhere," Bud told Violet over Sunday dinner. "I'm headed up there tomorrow morning. I'll leave here at 5:00. Don't want to miss the show."

Near 6:00 AM the next morning, Bud found his stakeout policeman who gave him the license plate number and the make of the car, a green Chevy, 1984. Bud called this information in to the Riverhead office. Having checked the data system, Bud received a call from his associate. The automobile was registered to one Alistair Williams.

The name rang a very loud bell!

Alistair and Scarlet Williams of Teaneck, New Jersey.

It had been almost a year ago – just before the November storm that took his house out to sea that Bud Rose had discovered the Williams pair in Montauk. Their real names, of course, were Sasha Annas and Jillian Burns. They had assumed false identities. They were on the run from the police because of their involvement in a car theft ring.

During the change of name and location, the two had become involved in pushing drugs! Now Alistair/Sasha was evidently back in that business big time.

Bud was on to him. It was only a matter of time. The Deputy Sheriff was elated.

Where was Jillian? She seemed to have disappeared into the depths of New York City. Bud was sure Sasha could solve the particular mystery of her whereabouts. They had been close as the proverbial thieves, pretending to be married – and from Teaneck, New Jersey yet? That last fact made Bud smile. Teaneck!

He knew he would now find Jillian. He would be able to keep her from trying to be part of the life of Starfish, her biological daughter from the sex-affair he had conducted with the woman before he married Violet.

That problem would be solved. He would be able to keep Starfish safely away from Jillian Burns who'd be in jail for her crimes, and what a relief!

Jillian Burns was one dangerous character.

Chapter Eighteen

SCHOOL DAYS

At the beginning of September, Starfish first went to school. Actually it was a pre-school, taking up only part of the day, morning through lunch (carefully nutritious) for the kids, and a nap, and then a play period.

Starfish would be two years old at Christmastime. She was precocious for her age – a little swimmer – already verbal – and with an innocence that protects. For these reasons, Violet had decided to enroll her in the pre-school called Toddlerville.

Violet would pick the child up at 3:00 in the afternoon and bring her back to her office in the Brandeis Realty building on Main Street, where Starfish had a playpen in an adjacent small room. It worked out well.

Toddlerville received its small clients in a house on Beach Lane in Westhampton Beach. Having Starfish there, safe, happy, and learning about colors and words and numbers, singing songs, identifying the animals in the Jungle Books, was so positive. The child thrived, and, her being so occupied, freed Violet to work in her office nearby for the better part of the workday.

Toddlerville was run by two youngish ladies who presided over a room of six toddlers ranging from one and a half years to three. The ladies were named Mrs. Tooey, and a Miss Elsie Jenkins who was engaged to be married and eager to get experience for the kids she expected to produce in the next few years.

They called her Star, Mrs. Tooey and Miss Elsie did. The other children all knew her parents called her Starfish – so when a kid taunted her, it never bothered her– for Starfish felt a special attachment to the sea, something she realized none of the other children had.

She was a Sea Star and her sense of belonging to the liquid world had been part of her since birth. When one of the little ones was jealous or angry with Star, he or she would whisper and giggle, 'Fishy', but this bothered her not at all, because she was a proud little girl, quite sure of herself, especially in terms of the sea. Sea Star. Starfish. She found it wonderful to bear such a name, a name belonging to no other child.

Life for Violet continued with work at the Real Estate office. Bud's peregrinations took him from one end of Suffolk County to the other. He was exceptionally busy in his hot pursuit of evildoers, Violet thought, with respect. Now, she was absorbed in her bright little daughter's early school days and Starfish was loving it.

Their world went on, among the Sea Stars and shining nights and cooler days. In spite of the violent ocean, which, like a recalcitrant woman with moods of sweetness and light, shifting to darkened depths, in spite of it, life was good.

Bud and Violet needed the sea, were devoted to it. Each was dependent upon it, as deeply as were the birds above the waves and the fish that lived within its belly. The Roses no longer lived right next to it, but in both their hearts, the water lapped. The ocean was always near. Starfish? She believed she was one of its waves or a drop of its salt, and she loved its briny taste.

In mid-September, the weather service announced to one and all that a tropical depression was in the south Atlantic and headed toward the East Coast of the United States. "Here we go again," was the attitude of Long Islanders. No one was unduly alarmed.

However, Violet was more than alarmed when she brought Starfish home on a cold September afternoon and announced, in the kitchen, "A lady came to see me today." The child spoke with a lisp.

"What kind of lady?" Violet was preparing chicken fingers and salad. Starfish loved the vinegary greens and Roma tomatoes.

"Oh, I don't know. She was tall." She picked a lettuce leaf out of its bowl and licked off the dressing.

Violet stopped, paused in middle of slicing a cucumber. "Tall! What do you mean tall?"

"Taller than Mrs. Tooey – and she's pretty tall for a teacher but Mrs. Tooey is fat."

"Was it at the school?"

"Uh huh, during recess. Boy, it was cold outside, but we're supposed to run around and get warm."

"Where were the teachers? Mrs. Tooey? Miss Elsie?"

"Oh, they were there outside with us."

"And they let this strange lady come up to you? You know I've always told you not to speak to strangers."

"Yes. But Miss Elsie came over with her and told me the lady knew my mommy and daddy."

Violet had crunched down beside her daughter. She turned the child toward her, hands on each of the small, rounded shoulders. She looked her straight in the eye.

"What did this lady say to you?"

"She said I was pretty." Starfish smiled with satisfaction. "Am I, Mommy?"

"Yes, darling." Violet's whole body was taut, expectant of horror. "What else did she say?"

"That my cheeks were so red." Starfish ate the lettuce leaf, "and that I had got bigger …"

"Have you ever seen this person before," Violet interrupted.

Starfish shook her head, still chewing on the lettuce.

"So she saw you in the playground during recess…today…?"

Starfish nodded again, then said, "What's the matter, Mommy? You look so pale."

"Nothing, darling. It's just…tell me anything else she said."

"She said she'd see me again… she wanted to get to know me, and that I looked just like a little rose, a little rosebud."

Chapter Nineteen

IN THE ACT

It was close to 7:00 AM that September morning, when a green Chevy, 1984 model, took a turn in front of The Clipper and came to a stop before its front door. Although it was too early for any barbering business, the lights in the building were on and the door unlocked.

Sasha Annas got out of the Chevy and went into the building.

"My God. He's got a moustache!" Bud Rose said. He was sitting in the unidentified car of the Islip cop – name of José. Bud's vehicle with Sheriff emblazoned on it, was parked on another street.

"Huh?" said José. "So? A moustache?"

"I know the guy. He looks different. But it's him all right." It was hard for Bud to believe the old Sasha could look so suave, so dapper. It wasn't just the moustache, which was slim above his upper lip. It was his whole demeanor – confident, almost graceful.

Then, Bud recalled that Sasha had been *Maitre d'* in the swanky Montauk Yacht Club dining room. He had evidently played the role well, including providing packets of smack surreptitiously to some of the elite members.

"I'll be damned," Bud said to himself. "He looks like a British fop!"

José looked at the detective. "Huh?"

"Nothing, José," Bud said as he saw Sasha emerge from The Clipper carrying a Publix paper bag, followed by a short guy – presumably Hal, the owner – with a second.

Sasha went to the back of his car, opened the trunk and the two bags were set inside. Sasha turned to Hal and presented him with an envelope, then moved to the front of the automobile. The two had not even shaken hands. There had been no parlay between them.

Bud was out of José's car and crossing the small parking area before Sasha noticed him. The Islip cop was right behind him, gun drawn.

"Sasha," Bud yelled. "Don't move."

All of Sasha's confident bearing crumbled in front of Bud's eyes. He looked to be the sniveling assistant at the King Kullen grocery chain in Eastport, in the old days, before Bud and Violet married.

"Fancy seeing you here," Bud said as he approached Sasha. Hal had rushed back into The Clipper and locked the front door.

Sasha just stood there wilting, even on a cold September afternoon, as José went around to the back of the building to try to apprehend Hal.

"Well, well, Sasha. Hey, I like the moustache. Suits you."

Sasha said nothing.

"Open the trunk," Bud demanded.

The two men went to the rear of the green Chevy. Sasha took his key and did as he was told.

"Take out the bags," was Bud's next order.

"What do you want me to do with them?"

"Follow me," and Bud led Sasha with his bundles to the next street and had him place the bags in the back seat of his Sheriff's vehicle. They went back together to The Clipper parking area and locked Sasha's car.

José, gun still drawn, emerged from the rear of The Clipper with Hal in tow.

"Take him over to your station for tonight, will you José? And send someone to impound this car." Bud tossed Sasha's keys over to José.

"Yes sir," José responded.

"I'll be up tomorrow to take over, okay?"

"Absolutely. By the way, Sheriff, good work."

"Same to you, José. See you *manāna*," said with a grin.

In the drive back to Riverhead, Bud put Sasha in the back seat with the two bags. He didn't want his brother-in-law to feel too cozy by sitting up front.

"How'd you get into this racquet, Sasha?"

"The usual way. Money."

"And your boss? He pays you well?"

"You could say so."

The answers from the back seat were sullen.

"We'll get more details about that boss tomorrow at the station."

"You already know. It's the same guy from Montauk."

"John Grunwald?"

"Oh, Christ. You didn't know?"

"I do now," Bud said, glancing in the rearview mirror to see Sasha's crestfallen face. "Tonight, my friend you will be sleeping behind bars."

There was silence from the rear. Sasha was looking out the window at the landscape flying by. He seemed unperturbed, but inside, thoughts racing, he had come to realize he was in deep, deep trouble. "I'm going to need a lawyer," he finally muttered.

"That you are, Sasha. That you are." Bud was driving fast. "By the way, where's your pal, Jillian or should I say Scarlet?"

"Don't know."

"You're not together anymore, Mr. and Mr. Alistair Williams?"

"Nope. I moved out of the place at 114th Street on the upper West side of New York a few weeks ago."

"Is she still there?" Bud's ears had pricked up. He would get the 114th address from Sasha tomorrow.

"I've no idea," Sasha said laconically. "Ask her Mom."

Bud said nothing. In fact, for the remainder of the drive, neither man spoke. It was beginning to rain, which only made things more depressing.

On his way back to Westhampton Beach from Riverhead, where he had incarcerated Sasha, Bud had stopped at Bide-A-Wee, the shelter where Lena and Gil had worked. He was able to get Gil's last address, phone number, and also the phone for his cousin Jake, at whose house apparently Gil spent many weekends.

Bud would find Gil Harrison, he was sure. Gil was still a kid, but surely an accessory in a death by overdosing. The youngster would probably get Juvenile Detention and certainly rehab.

It was a good day, Bud thought, a stellar day… Sasha behind bars… and his connection to John Grunwald confirmed. Sasha in all his consternation at being caught in the act had inadvertently confessed to their nefarious arrangement.

Hal! He was behind bars at the Islip Police Station for the moment, The Clipper closed. There was much work to be done there, finding his suppliers, but Bud was pumped up with the catch of two such vital actors in the drug case.

He couldn't wait to get home to Violet and a glass of Merlot – or two. He was all anticipation.

When he entered the house, he sensed right away that something was very wrong.

He found Violet on the couch in the living room. It was late enough that Starfish was in her room, not yet asleep, but getting there. By the look on his young wife's face, Bud knew there was a major problem.

He was yet to learn that Jillian Burns had come to town to stake a claim.

Starfish was in her sights. Starfish was her prey.

To Jillian, her motherhood was all she had. It would not be denied and Rose Bud – no more Starfish – would be back where she belonged!

Chapter Twenty
A COMMAND

"I need a lawyer. Ya gotta help me." It was Sasha on the phone to John Grunwald. Sasha was allowed one call and only one.

"Where are you?"

"Riverhead police station."

"They fingered you?"

"Yeah. Bud Rose."

"Christ! Not that fellow again. What'd you tell him?"

"Well it was all pretty obvious once they opened the trunk. I guess they had a stake out for some days."

"I asked you what did you tell them?" Grunwald's voice was ice cold. "About me?"

"I guess they'd already figured it out."

"You bastard. You ratted me?"

"No. No. They'd already made the connection."

"I don't believe you. Look, Sasha, this is big trouble…for both of us. I'm afraid you're on your own."

"You're not going to get me a lawyer?"

The words went into thin air because John Grunwald had already slammed down his receiver. "I gotta get out of here," he exclaimed in a loud voice.

Grunwald had chores to do. First: transfer money to a numbered anonymous account that only he could access at the Canadian bank in Montreal. Next: ready the yacht. Third: call his sister, Melinda. He didn't call his lawyer. He didn't want anyone to know he was gone, except for his sister, and she, he swore to silence.

Before doing anything more, he phoned his Captain.

"Willis, get your ass over here."

"Mr. Grunwald, I don't work for you anymore."

"You want to go to jail?"

"Looks like I may be headed that way," the Captain said ruefully. Then, he added in a soft voice, "and maybe you are too."

"No way, baby. Get over here, Richard." Suddenly the great man's voice was cajoling. "I need you, and you know what? You need me. We're both under the gun. We gotta get out of this mess together."

"And just how do you propose to do that?"

"*The Otellia.*"

"What?"

"You heard me. The yacht. You and I are going to take her for a ride... and I mean right now. Tonight."

"You've got to be kidding."

"And bring your passport."

"Mr. Grunwald. You're scaring me."

"Scared enough to refuse one million dollars?"

There was silence on the Captain's end. Then, he said in a low voice, "there's a real problem. The weather service is predicting a major hurricane coming up the East coast."

"A few waves," was the response.

"It's no joke, sir. They've even named it already –VIOLET. Hurricane VIOLET."

"It's barely started."

"They predict it being in the Carolinas by tomorrow morning."

"Okay, that's good. That gives us time to outrun it."

"Look, sir. There's a lot of turbulence and screwy weather preceding one of these babies."

"But you're a pro, Richard. You know that boat."

There was again silence on the Captain's end.

"I want you to come into Trump Tower right away. You should get here in a couple of hours. Then you and I will drive up to Mystic Marina.

I'll have the yacht gassed and ready in advance, put on some food, and we – you and I Richard – we'll beat the fucking storm!" He laughed, "and the fucking cops."

"I don't know…"

"Come on. A million bucks? And maybe a new life in Canada? Hey, I'm looking forward to it. Could be quite an adventure. How can you resist?"

"You don't know the ocean, sir."

"But you do." There was a pause. "It's a chance. We could be underway by midnight – if you leave Long Island now."

"Well…"

"I know you live alone, Richard – no ties – and just think of those beautiful Canadian broads."

John Grunwald could hear a chuckle on the other end, and he knew he was winning.

"Hey Richard, it sure beats jail time."

That did it, sealed the deal.

After Willis' arrival at Trump Tower at 5:30 that evening, Grunwald got into the Captain's automobile. He brought nothing with him but a small black case containing a passport, some banking records, an address book, and a wad of $100 dollar bills.

John Grunwald left the Tower in a sour mood, wearing dark glasses and a black fedora. It was not exactly a disguise, but it was certainly unusual attire for the tycoon. He did not wish to be noticed as he left New York City.

Once in the car, he removed both glasses and hat. His humor improved, and although they did not speak much on the journey to Mystic Marina in Connecticut, when they did, it was non-committal.

The Captain was tense. John Grunwald was not.

"Cheer up, old man," Grunwald finally commented. "You seem so uptight."

"I'm worried about the weather."

"A storm coming? You've been through more than one, haven't you, in past sailings?"

"Sure…but not hurricanes. At least not on purpose."

"Well, this one IS on purpose! What'd you say the name was?"

"VIOLET."

"VIOLET, eh? What a silly girly name. Huh. We're gonna beat the damn little pussy all the way to Canada. You'll see. We'll outrun the bitch."

There was silence for the rest of the way, as Grunwald leaned back in his seat. Just before he shut his eyes, he remarked in a sleepy tone, "Besides. Consider *The Otellia*. She's made of the best, the latest, most expensive equipment ever. She can stand any impact."

"The ocean doesn't care how she's built," Captain Willis mumbled. Head down, he drove as rapidly as the speed limit allowed on the Merritt Parkway. He was uncomfortably aware of the quickening winds and the rain drops of an early squall, as his hands clutched the wheel.

For good or ill, *The Otellia*, captained by Richard Willis, with his newly resurrected boss aboard, sailed north out of Mystic Seaport, Connecticut, near 11:00 PM that mid-September night on a dark and ominous sea.

Chapter Twenty-One
THE NOT-SO-EMPTY NEST

Bethany Brandeis felt she could not stay at the Cove another night! The emptiness, the lack of another whom she could pamper and cook for and make love with, brought a despair she had never experienced.

The charming house, which she had so artfully decorated and cherished, was now simply a building without a heart. She could stand it no longer and listed it for sale on the market at a very healthy price.

This meant she still had to stay in Montauk. As soon as The Cove sold, she could make her main place of residence, the Mill Road house in Westhampton Beach, which she had retained. Once back there, she determined she would spend as little time in Montauk hamlet as possible.

The Montauk branch of Brandeis Realty was doing an extremely swift business. Bethany had trained a number of sharp agents – three young woman and one older man – and they were more than capable of taking care of realty deals, open houses, lawyer contacts (no longer Augustus Brandt!) and the keys to the properties.

Bethany would make the trip to Montauk often enough to keep control. That was the plan. In the meantime, she had to stay put at The Cove. As it was September, the sale would be difficult. The time of year was bad for buyers of homes for summer use and pleasure. So Bethany was left to roaming the house at night, lying sleepless in the brass bed upstairs, and from time to time, weeping into the pillow, whispering his name.

How she dreaded running into Gus Brandt which could not help but happen in such a small town, particularly after the season ended. Even though she never went again to Shagwong's, 'their place', where after many a lunch, and always when dinner was done, the two of them ended up back at The Cove in the bouncy brass bed. It was cruel, no, quite unbearable.

When she would see Gus coming out of his office, or at the fishmongers, or leaving the hardware store, she would immediately cross the street or duck into a doorway. Sometimes he would have noticed her, start toward her with a ready smile, but so far, she had been able to elude any actual contact.

One cloudy September day, right before VIOLET hit Long Island, Bethany was in the local Fresh Market, picking up ripe tomatoes and broccoli and local strawberries, and with purchases in hand, turned and literally bumped into the tall man standing directly behind her. He had been there for a couple of minutes, waiting.

"Oh," escaped her.

"Hi, Sweetheart," Gus said. He was devouring her with his eyes, head to toe.

"Excuse me," she said shyly.

"No. I don't excuse you. I don't excuse you for not taking my calls. I don't excuse you for avoiding me at all costs. I don't excuse you for not letting me make love to you again."

"Please, Gus."

"We had it so good, baby," he said, his voice pleading, and for a moment all the torment, the longing, the desire flooded through her.

"I've got to go."

"Big date? You cooking dinner?" he said looking at her bags of vegetables. "Hey, I'll pick up a steak and – I love broccoli, particularly with *hollandaise*. Do you make it? I'll bet you do."

"Please let me get by."

"No, Bethany. How about tonight? I'm serious about a steak and being in that lovely house again with you…even if its only dinner. I've missed you, baby. I mean it." His sheer physicality engulfed her. He exuded that same old masculine vibe that had seduced her in the first place.

"Oh why not," she suddenly said, almost against her will. "Why not. You get the steak. I'll meet you there," and she turned to leave.

"I'll also get a bottle or two," Gus said. "Can't wait. *Hollandaise?*"

"Hollandaise," she answered with a smile that stayed with her as she drove home to The Cove. It was now pouring rain, and the wind howled, early manifestation that a storm named VIOLET was about to arrive, but Bethany did not notice the weather. In her mind, she was going over her recipe for *sauce* hollandaise.

Chapter Twenty-Two

BERMUDA?

It was a dark night. The waves began to look slicked with oil, under the headlights, as Captain Richard Willis maneuvered *The Otellia* forward against the wind. The seawater rose and fell with frightening force, each peak growing higher by the minute.

The storm, hurricane VIOLET, was equally as strong, or stronger, than ROSE had been in May of the year before, though later in the season. This was a mid- September event, rising up from the Caribbean, with a wind field of almost 900 miles. It had already killed people in its movement up the East Coast, mostly in northern Florida.

John Grunwald had no idea of this. He was oblivious, did not care, was truly obsessed with reaching a Canadian haven, safe from 'those fucking cops!'

Inside the elegant main cabin of the yacht, with its mahogany paneling and black leather sofas, Grunwald lolled on a lounge chair covered in a black and white checked fabric. He was well into the bottle of scotch he clutched in one hand. No glass with ice…no napkin…just the naked bottle, the liquor in it, reduced by half.

He was alone, his Captain in the front of the boat at the controls.

"He'd better steer this thing clear," he muttered, taking a large swig from the bottle in his hand. "He'd better get us to Canada – or else! No police… no jail time… just good old Canada. I can get lost in those woods and lakes easy. And Montreal, Toronto? Great towns. Lots of action. It's gonna be just fine!" and he took another swig, as *The Otellia* made a heavy swerve.

"Oops," Grunwald shouted. He was quite drunk. "Glad I transferred a bunch of money yesterday to BMO – the Bank of Montreal. Gonna come in handy."

John Grunwald was feeling no pain. He had no idea how precarious a situation his lavish boat was in. But Richard Willis did. The Captain was in a near panic, his discipline crumbling.

Alone, he was struggling, physically man-handling the tiller, which seemed to have a mind of its own as it turned the rudder of the boat from side to side. The sea, too, seemed to have its own violent agenda for *The Otellia*. Willis knew that did not make sense, but he had long captained, had been at the helm of many such small ships, and understood from the bottom of his soul, that the ocean had a will of its own.

From the intercom, he heard Grunwald's voice. "How's it going up there, Richard?"

"It's tough, sir."

"Hey, don't call me 'sir'. We're in this together as a team, right?"

"Right." The Captain just couldn't say 'John'.

"Whoops," Grunwald squealed into the intercom. "That was a big one!"

It was. A huge wave had hit the side of the boat and almost tipped it over.

"I can't be talking now," the Captain said quickly as he wrestled with the ocean, "but before I sign off, I think we should head for Bermuda."

"What? Bermuda? That silly little island? Don't fuck with me, Willis," Grunwald shouted. "I'm paying you to get me to Canada. I've got friends there – associates – guys I've done business with for years."

The captain could literally hear John Grunwald gulp down some liquid – presumably alcoholic from the sound of his boss's voice and the slurring of his words.

"According to the quadrants I am looking at, Bermuda will be out of the direct path of the hurricane. There will be turbulence, but the major threat is right here where we are, off the coast. It looks like it's aimed right up to Nova Scotia."

"That's part of Canada, right?"

"Always has been, sir. It's one of the provinces."

"That's where we're going, Willis. That's where *The Otellia* is headed. Not Bermuda, you got that? So it's a little rougher trip! So what? Bermuda is not an option."

"But sir…"

"That million bucks looks awfully iffy if we end up in Bermuda, Richard. In fact, it looks impossible. So you better make up your mind that Canada is our destination!"

"But…"

"Stop with the 'buts', Richard," Grunwald yelled. He was almost incoherent, his final words to his Captain, "Just shut up and steer!"

Chapter Twenty-Three

HOLLANDAISE

In the kitchen of The Cove, Bethany Brandeis was beating three egg yolks with a wire whip in a saucepan. She then beat in one tablespoon of lemon juice, one tablespoon of water, and salt and pepper. She had the pan beside the stove, readying the concoction to be slowly heated and incorporated with butter.

She was wearing the diaphanous red caftan that she had worn at her last miserable meeting with Gus, after the thong was discovered, when she threw him out of her house and her life unceremoniously.

Here she was, cooking for him again, excited beyond reason, but also, underneath, quite disgusted with her defenseless state...defenseless because she wanted him still. Oh, yes. That old feeling was still there. Her ambivalence was extreme, and she wondered how she could have let this *rendezvous* happen.

As she took two sticks of butter from the small refrigerator, and started to incorporate small pats into the beaten eggs in the saucepan under a low heat, there was a loud knock at the front door. She quickly turned off the stove.

Smoothing her hair, she almost ran, then, slowed to a seductive walk, to open the door to the man who had betrayed her and for whom she still yearned.

The wind nearly knocked her over, as she saw Gus, his shoulders hunched, his suit, even under the umbrella, wet from the pelting rain.

There was even water on his face, and in the light above the door, she could see his eyelashes glisten.

He had a huge grin on his face, and carried a steak in its wrapper in the hand that held his umbrella, and a bottle of champagne in the other.

"Home, again, Sweetheart. I'm home again."

"I don't know about that, Gus, but anyway, come in. Get out of the rain," Bethany said, turning from him. She was trembling.

"Wow," he said. "It's some storm out there. They say we're going to get a hurricane."

"No!" She turned back to him. "Really? A hurricane?"

"Yes. They've already named her VIOLET." He handed her the steak. "This is already cold," he said as he started to attack the cork at the top of the bottle of bubbly. "There's another one of these in the car."

"VIOLET," Bethany said. "Curious. Why VIOLET?"

"Apparently there have been a lot of named storms this year, just not on Long Island. The weather service just goes up the alphabet."

He went to the case where china was kept and selected two stemmed glasses. "You see I haven't forgotten," he said with a smile, waving the glasses at her. "Everything in its place…especially you!"

Bethany took the steak to the kitchen where the grill pan was already placed on a stove that was not yet turned on. She couldn't keep her hands from shaking as she placed the meat on a cutting board beside it.

Then, from behind, she felt his arms around her, his body pressing against her, his hands where they always went to arouse her, and just before she was lost to the rhythm of his movements, a huge gust of wind blew out the kitchen window, spreading glass shards across the floor and even onto the steak near the stove.

Bethany and Gus split apart, shocked by the suddenness of the explosive burst of wind and glass that had filled the kitchen. Gus had been cut slightly by a shard that had hit his chin. It was a tiny scratch but was bleeding. Bethany grabbed a towel and started dabbing at the blood, but then passed the cloth to Gus to do his own dabbing.

The act had seemed to her too suggestive, although what had passed between them just before the eruptive incident was far more intimate.

'Thank God,' she said to herself. 'We'd have been at it for sure if the wind hadn't blown away the moment.'

Gus was cursing as he attended to his face.

"I'll get a Band Aid," she said.

"No need," Gus said. " I think I've got it stopped." He went over to the window. The wind was still howling through its empty frame. Raindrops accompanied the gusts. The sill was soaked with water as were the white filmy curtains.

There happened to be a large, empty cardboard box in the corner of the kitchen. It had contained some appliances that Bethany had unwrapped that afternoon: a blender, a new toaster oven, and a Mr. Coffee, all equipment she felt a buyer of the house might appreciate because she planned to sell The Cove furnished. The new appliances might be a small enticement

Gus managed to pull apart the carton, and asking for a hammer and nails, which Bethany found in a side drawer of the pantry off the kitchen, he managed to tack up panels of cardboard, which at least kept the rain out temporarily.

"These won't last long. They'll probably blow out before morning. God. I sure didn't expect to spend the evening like this." Gus sounded so juvenile and whiney that Bethany was completely turned off.

"Sorry," she said in a sarcastic tone.

"Well, did you expect a night like this? You don't need to sound so cold."

"You act as if I planned this to happen."

"Sarcasm doesn't become you," he said.

"And petulance doesn't become YOU!" she exclaimed.

It was a bitter little exchange between the two.

Suddenly, they heard a crashing sound from the living room. They both ran in to find the china case turned over on the floor. Wind had come down the staircase next to it, which meant the bedroom window upstairs must have been blown open.

"Oh, God, Gus. Upstairs!"

He ran up and quickly returned. "It's a mess up there."

"What do you mean?"

"What'd ya think I mean?" His voice was nasty. "The bed's soaking wet. There's already water on the floor. Why in hell did you ever buy this place so close to the ocean?"

Bethany was stunned.

"I bought it because I loved it. I bought it as a …" she could not continue with the words like 'love-nest' or 'to be together with you in that wet brass bed' or 'for US'. The words would not come.

Bethany looked at him. His face was sullen, annoyed at all the inconvenience that the storm had wrought, at the interruption of his planned night of booze, steak, and sex. The knick on his face had formed an ugly scab.

For Bethany, all ambivalence she had felt was gone. Hurricane VIOLET had purged all desire for Gus from her heart and from The Cove. His disdain and downright nastiness had done it, and she felt clean.

The storm was not through. The next destruction to her property was outside. The steps upward from the beach, with its border of Montauk daisies, the entrance alcove at the door with its lattice and vines, all were ripped away and sea water lapped at the door of the house.

Electric power had been cut off. Bethany and Gus half lay on separate white sofas in the dark. She had brought out a couple of blankets, also some cheese and crackers and slices of salami, which they munched.

The champagne bottle was long emptied, but a bottle of Grey Goose vodka was on the coffee table between the two sofas.

They did not talk much, just listened to the wind howl and the ocean roar, nor did they sleep. It was just too noisy, too fraught with danger, and so the night passed.

Gus left as soon as morning light seeped into the living room. The wind had died down somewhat. "We may be in the eye of the storm," he said. "I'd better go while there's a break."

"By all means, go." And he did, sloshing out to his car. It was still raining, but less fiercely. When he stood beside his automobile, he turned and waved to Bethany who stood in the open doorway of The Cove. That was his goodbye.

Bethany shut the door and looked around the living room. The china case was still flat on the floor. The blankets were tossed aside, his in a wad, also on the floor. Empty glasses and bits of cracker crumbs were on the coffee table. "What a mess," she said out loud as she went into the kitchen. The wet cardboard had fallen from the window. The raw steak had bits of glass embedded. When she looked at the stove, Bethany let out a great laugh because what she saw seemed so appropriate.

The *Sauce Hollandaise* had curdled.

Chapter Twenty-Four
THE YELLOW PAD

Detective Flannigan and Deputy Sheriff Bud Rose were at the office of the missing John Grunwald in Trump Tower. They had a warrant.

Hurricane VIOLET had moved farther up the coast, but the streets of New York City were still wet and slippery and the rain still poured.

Both detectives were damp - hair, clothes, mood - as they went through the magnate's closets. They inspected his kitchen. They took apart his desk, where, there, on the leather top, was a yellow pad with three names, each with a New York City phone number. Heading the sheet were the words: Long Island Connection – Islip planes.

As it turned out, the names were of associates of Grunwald in the narcotics trade that he had contacted trying to find a Long Island supplier. Each had given him the same individual: Hal at The Clipper in Ronkonkoma near the Islip/ MacArthur Airport.

"This is one of those rare moments," Flannigan said, with the yellow pad in hand. "It happens once in a million years." His frame of mind was much improved by this discovery.

"Amazing coincidence," Bud exclaimed.

"No. Sheriff, it's not. It's fate. I believe in fate, do you?"

"I do now," Bud said with a laugh.

"I know all these names...never had cause enough to approach them – but I do now, particularly with Hal in custody. He must be known to all these guys."

"We've really got something to work with," Bud said.

"You mean some ONE," Flannigan responded. "Hal? The trouble is, it's just a dent, a bottomless pit. Sorry to mix metaphors. But there are always more to come."

"It's like playing whack-a-mole," Bud said.

Flannigan sat down behind the sumptuous desk. "I believe Grunwald had little family…I think a sister…yes, I'm sure a sister. Read about her on page six of The Post – some party where the sister and her husband… Her name is Melinda. I'm sure," Flannigan burst out. "And her hubby, Paul Felder – he's a developer too – yeah, Felder. That's right."

"You remember?"

"Yeah. I have a great memory for this kind of stuff. Sorry if I'm talking to myself…but I'm sure they live in Connecticut."

"Now, I'm remembering…Didn't Willis say Grunwald's yacht was taken up to Mystic Marina, when you had him there down town?"

"Absolutely. I'm going to call Melinda Felder and Captain Richard Willis right now."

It was easy enough to find the home numbers on the computer next to the desk. Flannigan dialed Melinda Felder. She answered. Flannigan put it on open mike.

"Mrs. Felder?"

"Who's this?"

"Detective Flannigan of the New York Police Department."

"Really!"

"You sound skeptical, Mrs. Felder, but I can assure you this is on the up and up. In fact, I am calling from your brother's office."

She paused, then, "How can I help you?"

"Do you know where you're brother is?"

"No. No I don't."

"When did you last speak with him?"

"A couple of weeks ago…before the storm."

"You mean VIOLET?"

"Is that what they named it? I guess so. Yes."

"What did you talk about?"

"He said he was going up to Canada…business stuff. He's done a lot up there," she added proudly.

"Do you know if he went?"

"Yes, he did. He told me not to tell anyone."

"Well, you've already told me," Flannigan said with a smile in his voice.

"Oh, so I have, detective."

"Did he go to Canada and if so where. It's a big country."

"Probably Montreal. That's where he does his Canadian banking."

"How did he get there?"

"He took the yacht."

"He went by boat?"

"Yes. His yacht *The Otellia.*"

"That's crazy! And this was right before the storm?"

"The night OF the storm," she corrected Flannigan. "I told him he was nuts to take it out when a big blow was coming. He said there was still time – that he and Captain Willis could outrun it."

"And did they?"

"I don't know. I haven't heard from him, but that's not unusual when he's doing business in Canada, a foreign country. Why, I hardly heard from him at all when he was in Europe. For six months yet!"

"If you hear from him, please call me," and Flannigan gave her his contact number and closed out the call.

"What'd you think?" Bud asked.

"Look. She's Grunwald's sister. How can you trust her?"

"You can't."

"Just a dent," Flannigan said as the two prepared to leave Grunwald's office.

"Yeah. Like playing whack-a-mole. You can't ever win."

"Depressing thought," Flannigan said. "Let's get out of here." They left the Tower together. The city was drenched, only to dampen still further the mood of each, as they walked out in the still pouring rain.

Chapter Twenty-Five

THE LAST OF *THE OTELLIA*

It was the worst storm of the century so far, was VIOLET, a quixotic tempest with odd eddies and lashing waves.

The Otellia plunged into the cold waters of the Atlantic, amidst unruly winds and swelling water. The men who sought to brave the wildness, at the very least, should expect bruises.

John Grunwald and Captain Richard Willis got far more than black and blue from forces known to crush and kill. They stared down a dark engulfing wave, an implacability that would sweep away all they had ever loved and life itself.

The moon was a sliver of lemon – a half lemon slice – when it could be glimpsed through the swirling clouds. It shone a pale light on a dire situation, a flailing ship, now close to an unforgiving shore.

The Otellia was lying on its side. *John* Grunwald had clambered over the tilted side of his yacht and dropped onto a mushy mix of sand and algae. It was pouring rain. He was up to his knees in seawater. Bleary, disoriented, he stood there drenched and furious. He was a big man, a heavy man. He raised his fist to the sky and cursed mightily – the earth, the sea, the cops, every woman he had ever known, the drug dealers and lawyers and Canadians. Most of all, he cursed Captain Richard Willis for putting him there, lost in the muck. The wind and sea called to John Grunwald as if they wanted him, and in the end, they won.

The sand beneath him began to sink beneath his feet, beneath his fury. John Grunwald was literally being sucked into the silt at the bottom of the ocean. It was not actual quick sand, but the seawater eddies had eroded sections of earth beneath the water line that left pockets deep enough to swallow a man.

He grew lower and lower, water seeming to rise, although it was actually he who was sinking. He was screaming curses the entire time, even until the salt water filled his mouth and nostrils and finally, stilled his voice.

For good.

The roof of the ship had been blown off completely by the wind. Willis was still clutching the helm, though lying on his side. Water was gushing from every direction. It wasn't long before his hands gradually released their grip, and half-conscious, Richard Wills slipped away to a watery grave.

The Otellia wreckage sank to the bottom of the Atlantic, but for a few pieces of wood that were found some days later near Bar Harbor Maine. One was the rear of the boat with its name imprinted in fancy letters: *The Otellia.*

The Maine Coast Guard checked the database and learned that the yacht was registered in Mystic Connecticut in the name of John Grunwald.

The week before the end of September, a piece of a club chair was found as far north as Yarmouth, Nova Scotia. It had floated all the way over The Bay of Fundy. Two boys, walking along the rocky beach had discovered the object, were delighted with its black and white checked fabric covering, now sodden but in tact. They took it home as a souvenir of what they did not know. Another week elapsed before the Maine Coast Guard notified the proper authorities in Connecticut and New York City.

It wasn't until the first of October that John Grunwald was officially declared dead, drowned during the storm, VIOLET. There was a sizeable obituary in The New York Times, and a column in The Post describing Grunwald's considerable social life.

Captain Richard Willis had died too, but there was only a small paragraph about him in The Southampton News, the paper in the town where he was born.

Chapter Twenty-Six

REAL ESTATE

Hurricane VIOLET cut a swath. A northern wall of water, created by winds that pushed the surge, created a wildly unpredictable tempest. The sand when the waves retreated was left ridged and rippled. A wild fog prevailed at times, until there was a final ray of light that revealed the devastation.

George Annas' stilt house had been standing since the 1940s. After VIOLET, it was no longer there, just four metal poles sticking up from the sand. This broke the old man's heart. Somehow he felt he had lost identity.

The stilt house had been unique for years, a stalwart little building against the elements, defying the neighboring mansions.

The House on the Hill lost shingles and many trees were down, blocking the street below. Throughout the storm, the family, Bud, Violet, Starfish, and Mookie, hunkered down in the basement, until it began to flood. VIOLET'S heavy rain seeped through the old framework of The House on the Hill. They were able to go upstairs when the water got deep because the worst of the storm was over.

When the basement was finally drained, the mold that developed made it necessary to remove all the sheet rock and rebuild the place, which Violet and Bud had previously used as a den and TV room. Once restored, it became a neat little apartment for George and Anastasia Annas to live in.

"You have to join The Swordfish Club, Dad," Violet insisted. The

Club was on Dune Road, directly next to where the stilt house had been. "I know how you miss living by the sea."

George spent many a long day at The Swordfish near his beloved ocean, where he brought his little granddaughter after her school day to swim in the wavelets at the edge of the sand, even into the fall and starting again in early spring.

The Cove also lost shingles, and had major water damage to the interior. The path from the beach and the alcove entrance had to be rebuilt. But of all the many structures on that part of the Montauk waterfront, The Cove, an older wooden house, survived better than most. Perhaps it was because it was low in height, had no deck facing the ocean, as many beach houses did, and somehow the wind blew right through its windows.

Other houses made of cement were tumbled to the ground by the force of the gusts against their solid mass.

The Bethany Brandeis Real Estate office, Montauk branch, was having difficulty in making sales after VIOLET. Buyers were cautious. Bethany had taken The Cove off the market. She loved the place, and since the Gus obsession was closed and defeated, she cherished The Cove even more. She was refurbishing its already singular charms with calico slipcovers and bright pillows, a canopy over the brass bed in the window upstairs, and the new kitchen appliances were put to good use. She had decided to live there on a regular basis and put her Mill Road house in Westhampton Beach up for sale.

"If The Cove could survive VIOLET, when so few other houses could not, I'd be a fool to ever let it go," she told those in her office.

Some who came to look for property, later, during the winter months, as the summer of 1987 approached, wished to see The Cove because they had heard of its charms and that it had been listed.

To these people, Bethany would say proudly, "Oh No. That was then – last fall. It's been pulled off the real estate market since hurricane VIOLET. The Cove easily withstood the storm," (as Bethany had been able to withstand Augustus Brandt!)

The last words were not quite true, but whatever there had been between the two was over for good. She had not seen him since the last vision of him, sloshing in water up to his knees to his car at the rear of The Cove driveway and his feeble wave goodbye.

John Grunwald's Cullodon Point home, although on a hill, was inundated with water because the vast, glass front window was destroyed at the outset of the storm. The pelting rain seemed to have taken dead aim at the house. Everything inside, all the expensive leather furnishings, the valuable paintings on the walls, the crystal chandelier – now in pieces on the sodden hardwood floor – all, were ruined. In what was left of the front patio, trash from across the bay had been washed up – a bag of onions, a child's teddy bear, even a mattress, all human detritus.

Gurney's Inn had lost its whole front deck with the umbrella tables. Bud Rose remembered how he had enjoyed their superior lobster roll. "The best I ever ate," he had exclaimed.

The long wharf at the end of Gurney's Beach was no longer there. It had been dockage for yachts and speedboats, including *The Otellia* – for parties aboard on sunny days – and the unloading of illegal drugs in the dark of night. The wharf's wooden planks were now on the bottom of the Atlantic. Some weeks after VIOLET, the U.S. Army Corps of Engineers cleaned up the area, along with much other debris from her destructive path.

The Montauk Yacht Club also had massive losses. The deck, with its fire-pits, so glamorous for an evening drink under the setting sun, had been swooped away by the raging waves. Many a Tequila Sunrise or Extra Dry Martini had been consumed on that deck by the elite guests, such as the Jordan Mathers of Quogue. "It's best we go into the dining room, Jordan," his wife Janice would remark after the third drink, "while we can still make it." The Montauk Lighthouse replica that stood in Lake Montauk, the Yacht Club's signature, had also been swept to sea.

VIOLET had reached Stella Burns' house in East Moriches. It was badly beaten, by the winds, and the old barn at the back of the property was completely destroyed. Stella had to get a neighbor with a tow truck to pick up the lumber off the ground and dispose of it…at a sizeable cost. "Scrounger," she called after the man, as he left with his load – and his money. "Talk about an out-and-out crook," she yelled.

As for Joe's Warm-Up Bar in the hamlet of Montauk, the fact

that the low building was nestled between two tall structures, saved the little bar from grave damage. In spite of the deluge of rain and the howling winds, at the height of the storm, Joe's Warm-Up was filled with fishermen telling ribald stories. "Who could go fishing in this weather?" one of the leathery-faced seamen would yell, and the answer from the group of drinkers would be in unison, "Not me!" in a loud chorus. Joe, the owner was pleased with the crowd. Luke, one of the locals, in his smelly slicker and filthy, scale encrusted boots, was holding forth. He reeked of fish as did his audience, who were downing pint after pint, and shot after shot, giving credence to the local joke, "Montauk's a drinking town with a fishing problem."

Chapter Twenty-Seven

SHOCK

Violet had been only six years old when she first saw a Nor'easter hit Westhampton Beach that caused damage and death. In a house that was uprooted and taken out to sea, she had heard the wails of the persons inside and the sound of a child's cry, a sound that stayed with her for her lifetime. So the cry she heard on the beautiful October Saturday morning in 1986 – her own child's voice – sent chills through her.

Violet heard it from inside the house. It was a haunting sound, a sound out of lost memory. And then there was the barking.

She ran from the kitchen to the top of the steps leading down to the back garden where Starfish had been playing with Mookie. Starfish had early on been afraid of the large animal. He would chase her. He was bigger than she, but now that she was at least as tall as he, they had become the best of friends, dog and child. The animal had grown almost as devoted to Starfish as he was to Bud, but not quite. Bud was the master of Mookie's love.

Starfish was nowhere to be seen, and Mookie was at the gate of the fence barking wildly. Violet fainted. She lay prone on the grass. The dog came to her and lay down beside her, his head next to hers. That's where Bud later found them.

Chapter Twenty-Eight

STELLA'S DILEMMA

"Jillian, what were you thinking?"

"I want what's mine."

"This little girl doesn't even know you."

"That can be fixed with time," Jillian said smugly.

"Can't you see she's miserable? Just look at that face."

Starfish was in a crumpled ball in the corner of the sofa, her eyes full of tears, mouth turned down. It was such a picture of fear – the clenched hands, feet pulled up into a near fetal position. The child was obviously terrified.

Stella Burns was beside herself. She was not a young woman, in fact quite aged for her years. Arthritis beset her, and she was given to frequent headaches. The thought of raising her granddaughter by herself was overwhelming.

"You think you're leaving her with me?" Stella exclaimed. "Well, girl, you think again. No way! I am just not up to taking care of an active toddler…"

"Mom, she's your own flesh and blood!" Jillian interrupted.

"And she's yours too. Think of her happiness. You're so selfish."

"Selfish am I?" Jillian snorted. "Look, I HAVE to leave her with you. There's no way I can take care of her in a tiny little flat on the upper West Side of New York City. God, Mom. I have to work!"

"Selfish, selfish, selfish. You kidnap her, rip her away from her family, then drop her off with me to raise, and you go on your merry way… Selfish is the perfect word for you."

"I'll be coming to visit often."

"Yeah, sure, once every six months maybe!" Stella said this with such disdain, Jillian grew angry.

"And just what kind of mother are YOU?" Jillian shouted.

"Now, calm down, Jill. This isn't going to work out. This kid belongs with her father and Violet. They are the parents she has always known."

"Well it's now time she knows her real mother," Jillian said, and she approached the child quite menacingly. Starfish winced and let out a little cry.

"What's to cry about, sweetheart?" Jillian said, plopping down next to her. "You're old enough to know the truth and who you really are. My Rose Bud."

Large tears were rolling down the cheeks of Starfish in her corner of the couch.

"Aw, stop with the weeping, Rose Bud. Be a brave little girl," and Jillian reached out a hand to touch her knee. The child recoiled.

Jillian sat back, annoyed. "Say something. I'm not going to bite you." The two stared at one another.

Stella, who was behind the sofa, came around and stood before them. "Leave her alone, Jillian. You're only making things worse."

Starfish had not moved, but now, she brushed away the tears on her cheek with her hand and in a tremulous voice, whispered directly at Jillian, "Who are you?"

For a moment, this startled the woman on the couch. She didn't speak, then, in a cranky voice, Jillian said, "I told you. I'm your real mother. You'd better get used to the idea, kid." Her tone had turned nasty.

Then, pointing to Stella, Jillian went on, "and this is your grandma."

"I know my grandma," Starfish said so softly, she could hardly be heard. "Grandma's nice to me."

"And I suppose I am not?" Jillian said, really annoyed.

"I don't even know you," the child responded, and she started to cry again.

"Oh stop with the waterworks! For God's sakes! This is too much!" and she rose to her feet. "I've got to get going, Mom. Not much of a visit, I know, but I have a job in the city. You notice I brought stuff for the kid. It's in this tote," and she dropped a large black bag in front of her mother.

"You're serious," Stella said, nonplussed.

"Of course. And by the way, should the good Deputy Sheriff have any questions about me, don't you dare breathe a word – much less about Rose Bud."

"I'll have to tell him, Jill."

"You want me to go to jail?" Jillian shouted.

"No, no, of course not, but this just isn't right."

"It's right for me."

"I told you that you're selfish."

"So be it," Jillian said. She kissed Stella on the cheek, bent over the cowering child and caressed her hair. Starfish ducked her head. "Oh come on, kid, what about a little affection." Starfish curled up into a ball again, hiding her face, closing her eyes.

"Well, have it your way, but just you wait, Rose Bud. Get used to it. Get used to me! We're going to be the best of friends. Just you wait."

The little girl winced. "Don't call me Rose Bud. I'm Starfish."

"Not for long," Jillian said, her tone raw. She went to the front door. "See ya, Mom. I'll call you in a few days. I'm taking your car again." and she was gone.

Chapter Twenty-Nine

GRANDMA

Stella was in shock when Jillian left so blithely. Here she was, alone with a distraught little girl. She could only go to her on the couch and fold her into herself. The child, her limbs entangled, gradually relaxed in her grandmother's arms and the sobs started.

Stella let her cry. "Poor baby," she whispered. "It's going to be okay, baby. I promise you. You'll see."

Stella held Starfish for many minutes this way until the sobs receded and the child fell asleep. She laid her carefully down, threw a small blanket over her and went into the kitchen to prepare something for Starfish to eat.

"Spaghetti?" she said out loud. "Yes. I know she loves it with just butter and cheese," and she set the pot to boil on the stove.

Sitting on a straight chair by the sink, Stella contemplated the dilemma she faced: what to do with Starfish? She knew that the little child was too much for her to care for by herself. Should she get a nanny? Jillian would have to pay for that. "I just can't afford such an expense."

Stella was still speaking out loud, as she often did. She figured it was part of getting old – that's what she told herself - and anyway, she liked the sound of her own voice. "Starfish has been at a pre-school. She told me she loves it, has other kids to play with, and she likes her teachers. She loves lunch there – sometimes hotdogs – sometimes pizza. There must be a local pre-school in East Moriches."

Stella was tapping her foot. "Ah, no," she said. "It's too much. Jillian should never have laid this on me!"

It was then she heard a cry from the living room, which made her start running.

Starfish was bolt upright on the couch. Her face looked frightened. "Baby, what is it?"

"I had a bad dream," the little girl said in a choked voice. "Mommy was gone. I couldn't see her and there was this black shadow..." Starfish stopped for a moment. Then, "I want my mommy. And I want daddy. Please, Grandma, I want to go home," these last words a wail, accompanied by further sobs and buckets of tears.

For Stella, this was the decision point.

She went to Starfish, took her in her arms and said, "Don't you worry. I'll call your daddy right away. Then we'll sit down and have some spaghetti with butter and cheese, just the way you like it, and wait for him to come and get you. Okay?" She looked down into Starfish's upturned, wet face. She had stopped crying.

"Oh, yes, Grandma. Please call my daddy. And spaghetti? Can I have ketchup?" For the first time, the child smiled. "I'm hungry."

The two sat at the kitchen table and ate their lunch with gusto, Starfish back to her chattering little self, with stories of playmates and Mookie, the dog, and how she loved to sit on the beach with the ocean at her feet.

"Do you really swim?"

"Oh, yes. I can, but not far. Sometimes it's like the waves get up on their hind legs and walk across the land - just like Mookie, the dog...on his hind legs. The water towers over me." Starfish said this with great pride. "But I'm never afraid."

"Perhaps you should be, darling. The ocean is a mighty force," said Stella soberly. "Now," as she took the empty dishes to the sink and went to the telephone on the sideboard, Stella announced, "I'm going to call your Dad."

She had to squelch her inner thought, 'what in hell am I going to say to Jillian?' as she picked up the receiver.

Chapter Thirty

BACK AND FORTH

Bud had arrived at Stella Burns' house within an hour of her call to him. He had dropped everything, left Riverhead, siren blazing and reached East Moriches to find his little girl, swathed in her grandma's arms.

Starfish let out a yelp when she saw her daddy.

"Stella, thank God." Bud was effusive, hugging the older woman, who still held the child. "I know this must have cost you a lot. Your daughter…" and he shook his head vigorously.

"I can't even think of Jillian at this time. She was wrong to kidnap this child. I told her how selfish she was, and of course she was furious. She had grabbed my car keys to go down to Remsenburg before I knew it and came back with Starfish who was bawling."

"Not your fault, Stella. God bless you for calling me. Violet's been frantic, as have I."

"Oh, poor Violet. I hope you've called her."

"Of course." Bud had taken Starfish into his arms. She lay against his chest, her breath coming in small heaves, but her tears had dried. He kissed the top of her head and that brought the first real smile she'd smiled in a couple of days. "Ready to go home, baby?"

"Yes, Daddy. Oh please." And she buried her face in his neck.

"Thank grandma for taking care of you and for calling me on the phone."

Starfish leaned over and put her cheek next to Stella's, which brought a tear to the older woman's eye. "Thank you, Grandma."

"You know you're always welcome here, Starfish. I'll keep you safe," a pledge she wasn't even sure she could keep, with Jillian poised to attack and almost unhinged.

"As Bud set Starfish down on the floor and took her hand to walk to the car, he asked Stella, "Where is she?"

"She has an apartment in New York on 114ᵗʰ Street. I'll get you the address," and Stella went over to the desk, wrote on a notepad and returned to give the slip of paper to Bud.

"This can't be easy for you, Stella."

"It isn't," and she burst into tears. "Go, go now, before I get all sentimental," and Stella virtually pushed them out the front door.

After dropping Starfish in the arms of her mother at the Brandeis Realty office a little before noon, Bud turned his Sheriff's car toward New York City and 114ᵗʰ Street. He did not realize that Jillian Burns was already driving back to East Moriches in her mother's car plotting her next step.

Stella had called Jillian to tell her she had returned Starfish to Bud Rose where the child belonged.

Jillian was outraged, filled with fury at her mother, but hid it carefully. Oh, Mom," she said. "I understand. A little girl is a lot to take care of. Let me come out and see you."

"Okay, Jillian, if you like." Stella was placated, unaware of the deep anger that possessed Jillian – anger towards her! "When?"

"Today?"

When the two Burns women were together in the East Moriches house, Jillian at first was solicitous, even kind. "You didn't get too much damage from VIOLET, Mom. I see some shingles need repair, and the front stoop."

"I was lucky. Lots of trees down in the street, and of course, the back barn, where I used to park the car, is completely gone."

"I see," said Jillian looking out the back window of the kitchen, while her mother was preparing coffee and sweet rolls for the two of them.

"Yeah. The old buggy is open to the weather. I'm not even allowed to park it on the street."

The two women sat down at the small table. Stella poured two cups. The plate of rolls was between them. After a bit of eating and drinking, Jillian asked her mother, "What did Bud say?"

"He was mighty relieved, of course. He said Violet was frantic."

"I'll just bet!" Jillian smirked.

"How can you make such a face? Of course she was frantic. Any mother would be."

"Except she's NOT a mother."

"It's the only one Starfish knows. It's time you realized that, Jill."

At this, Jillian rose to her feet, slamming down the sweet roll, which she had crumbled in her fist. "That does it! You're always rooting for Bud."

"That's not fair, Jill."

"Then how could you have given my child back to that bastard? You know how I hate him – how I hate the two of them, him and his precious doll-wife, Violet?" She started to pace.

"Just calm down, Jill. You know you and your blood pressure. Don't be so upset. You gotta realize both Bud and Violet are doing their best for Starfish and she loves them."

That was the *coup de grace*.

"Loves them," Jillian screamed. "Loves them."

She approached her mother who was sitting there, appalled by this outburst. Jillian was menacing. "I'm going back to Remsenburg."

"What?"

"You heard me. I've still got your keys."

"No, no, now come on, Jill. Not again."

"As long as it takes, Mom."

"No Jill. Don't snatch that child away for a second time - and so soon!"

"I swear…" Jillian's fist was raised over her mother's face. The two were frozen in time.

"You wouldn't!" Stella was appalled.

"Oh yes I would, old woman." Stella sat immobile, pale as death.

"Aha. Got 'em," Jillian said. "They're right here in my purse. Mom, Rose Bud is the only thing in my whole life I ever got right!"

"Oh Jill…" Stella sat there devastated.

"And I'm going to get her now. For good!" She stood for a moment before her mother. "You've never been on my side, never!"

"Oh Jill. I've only wanted the best for you, always."

"Sure, Mom, sure." Jillian gave her a look of such disdain, Stella gasped. "By the way, thanks for the sweet roll. Think I'll take another," and grabbing a sticky bun, Jillian sauntered out of the kitchen door to the back of the lot.

Stella, from her chair, could see through the window her daughter get into her car and with bumpy movements, drive away over the muddy grass toward the street. She sat at the table in tears, next to the plate of sweet rolls and the dirty coffee cups, until it turned dark outside.

Chapter Thirty-One

CONFRONTATION

It was late in the afternoon, as Violet finished painting the outdoor chairs on the back patio. They had been left out by mistake during the storm, VIOLET, and although in tact, looked weather beaten in the truest sense.

As it was October, she wore a sweater and jeans under her smock, which swirled about her, as she wielded the brush with blue paint for its last strokes.

"There," she said with satisfaction. "That's better, isn't it darling?" this addressed to Starfish who was sitting at a small table, bundled into a puffy coat. The child was using crayons to fill in images in her coloring book – dogs, rabbits, birds. Mookie was at her feet, protective.

Starfish looked up and smiled at her mother. "Good," she said nodding her head at the brightly painted chairs. Then, with a little cry, she said, "Look!"

Violet turned, and in the shadow of the house, there stood a dark figure. It remained immobile for a moment, then stepped forward into the dimming afternoon light and spoke. "I saw Bud leave in his car."

"Jillian!"

"You got it, Violet. Jillian Burns, here to take back what's hers."

"You've been lurking in the bushes?" Violet exclaimed.

"Just biding my time," Jillian tossed off.

"I saw her at my grandma's," Starfish wailed.

"That you did, baby," Jillian said. "I told you then it was only the beginning for you and me."

"How dare you," Violet said, coming toward her unwanted guest.

"Oh, that's good, Violet. I have every right..." and with that, Jillian stepped close to Violet and slapped her hard in the face.

Violet recoiled, shocked, furious. She returned the blow.

It became a battle royal between the two, physically and mentally. Starfish cowered under the awning on the terrace, while her two mothers, one biological, the other emotional, came to blows in front of her.

Mookie, the German shepherd, was at the child's feet, alert, tense. At the moment he did nothing but glare with his amber eyes and curl his lips to show his teeth. The dog was on the ready for anything. His whole attitude was 'don't you dare come near my little one.'

Jillian Burns, in recent months, had gained weight. Her working conditions did not allow for much movement. She had never been into exercise. That, and all the take-out meals, had added poundage.

Violet was smaller, slimmer. Swimming against the tides had kept her legs and arms strong and lean. She was agile.

The two women were face to face, each with hands on hips. Their eyes were locked in hatred, one against the other. Jillian suddenly pulled Violet's blond hair.

Violet responded by yanking at Jillian's ponytail.

Starfish cried out "Mommy," at which both women looked at her.

"This is ridiculous," shouted Violet.

"You've always had it all," Jillian shouted back.

"You mean Bud!"

"I had him first," Jillian shrieked.

"Yeah, for sex, period. He never loved you...not for a minute."

This enraged Jillian. She turned red. "Look what I produced...what I gave him," and she went toward the child at which Mookie stood up and growled. He was a frightening presence. Jillian paused, scared.

"Yes, you produced her, as you so crassly put it. But that's all you did. You didn't even want her. Neither did Bud in the beginning. But now Starfish is the love of his life."

"Rose Bud! Don't you dare keep calling her Starfish. It's not even a name."

"It is too," the little girl called out. Starfish was beginning to find the fight between her mommy and this strange lady curious and interesting. She, of course, hadn't the least idea of what was going on, but it was intriguing to see two adult females so uncontrolled and raw, particularly her mommy.

Violet was always so calm and quiet with her daughter, so affectionate and easy. Starfish had never seen her unleashed in this way and SO angry.

"What's the matter, Violet? You want Rose Bud because obviously she's the only child you're ever going to have!"

"Oh, really?"

"Your sex life with Bud is apparently a bust. You're the kind of woman that just lies there, I'll bet. Poor Bud. Well, he knows where he can get the real sugar…and I don't mean White Sugar." Jillian was sauntering around the fieldstone-floored terrace. She had taken hold of a spade that was leaning against the outer door of the house and was swinging it from side to side.

Mookie was in a crouch, ready to spring, lips drawn back, showing all his teeth, and the growl that emanated from him was deadly serious. He didn't take his eyes off the woman with the spade.

This caused Jillian to stop in her tracks, but she held on to the lethal weapon. "You know, I don't really need this. I'm big and strong enough to take you on all by myself," she yelled over at Violet.

"My Mommy's bigger and stronger than you are," Starfish yelled back. "They even named a hurrycane after her. Hurrycane VIOLET!"

This brought a nasty laugh from Jillian. "Hurrycane!"

It was at this moment that Bud Rose appeared, coming around the corner of the house.

"Well, well," he said calmly. "If it isn't Jillian. Hey, I've been looking for you."

"You're back so soon?" Jillian quavered.

"Yep, and evidently just in time," he said, taking the spade from her hand.

"I had a little errand at the pharmacy."

"Is someone ill?" Jillian asked, placating.

"Just some medication, for morning sickness," Bud said, as he gave a small packet to Violet.

"What?" Jillian's mouth dropped.

"And I've got something for you too, Jillian," Bud continued, as he pulled a pair of handcuffs from his back pocket.

"You wouldn't," Jillian cried out again. "Bud. It's me…It's Jillian. You used to call me you're 'favorite sport'. Don't you remember?" Tears were streaming down her face.

"That was another life, in a far off time. You've been a busy girl since then, haven't you, Jillian? Car theft. Pushing drugs. Mrs. Alistair Williams from Teaneck, New Jersey?" Bud said the last words with relish. "I'm afraid, Jillian, you're going away for a long, long time."

"You wouldn't do that to me," she screamed as he turned her around.

"Oh, yes I would." He clamped the cuffs over her wrists.

"I'm mother of your baby, Bud. I gave you Rose Bud."

"Starfish is mine. Starfish is Violet's, and by the way," he added. "Violet and I are having twins…boys. She'll have two little brothers."

Jillian left with a howl, as Bud was leading her to his car at the front of the house to drive to the Riverhead precinct. As he turned the corner, in the quickening dark, Bud turned back to his wife, blew her a kiss and said, "I'll be right back, darling. This," and he indicated Jillian, "is the end of a chapter."

Case closed.

EPILOGUE

The storm that hit Long Island, dubbed VIOLET by the Federal Weather Service, was the largest so far. Why is it so often a woman's name? Is the female as unfathomable as the ocean's depth?

It stretched more than 900 miles across. The winds hit 190 miles an hour in velocity. The water in bays and oceans, lakes and ponds, rose prodigiously. In New York Harbor, the waves reached over 40 feet. Even Lady Liberty, standing tall, was damaged during the storm. The repairs to her structure took many months after the winds and rain came to an end.

Violet Rose was not flattered by the storm's name. She was terrified. As years passed, the violence of the ocean had grown perceptibly in strength and destruction. No one was safe anymore. Few buildings could survive. Animals – from pets to wild ones- could not escape.

Neither could people.

Herman Melville wrote of the sea: "That deep, blue bottomless soul" an ocean metaphor for those that live above, around, and in the ocean.

And Homer called it "the wine dark sea" when he spoke of the Aegean.

Water from the melting icecaps, softening glaciers, and breaking frozen plateaus, one day may consume the world that we know. Climate change and global warming are caused in part, by the most violent of animals, we, members of the human race.

Climate change is a destroyer. It also traffics in disruption, disarray, increasingly frequent and more powerful storms and droughts, heightened flooding, and stretches of inhospitable heat. Yet water is the ultimate force, churning like so many lives.

Long Island was covered with water during VIOLET – from the Atlantic Ocean to Long Island Sound. Across the flat surface of the landmass that has few hills, the salt water flowed, but it did not sink Long Island.

Not yet.

But when?

Printed in the United States
By Bookmasters